Dan Neil

THE
KILLING JARS

TRAFFORD

USA ▪ Canada ▪ UK ▪ Ireland

Note for Librarians: A cataloguing record for this book is available from Library and Archives
Canada at www.collectionscanada.ca/amicus/index-e.html
ISBN 1-4120-9497-6

Printed in Victoria, BC, Canada. Printed on paper with minimum 30% recycled fibre.
Trafford's print shop runs on "green energy" from solar, wind and other environmentally-friendly power sources.

Offices in Canada, USA, Ireland and UK

Book sales for North America and international:
Trafford Publishing, 6E–2333 Government St.,
Victoria, BC V8T 4P4 CANADA
phone 250 383 6864 (toll-free 1 888 232 4444)
fax 250 383 6804; email to orders@trafford.com
Book sales in Europe:
Trafford Publishing (UK) Limited, 9 Park End Street, 2nd Floor
Oxford, UK OX1 1HH UNITED KINGDOM
phone 44 (0)1865 722 113 (local rate 0845 230 9601)
facsimile 44 (0)1865 722 868; info.uk@trafford.com
Order online at:
trafford.com/06-1252

10 9 8 7 6 5 4 3

DEDICATION

For Mom and Pat. Just a breath away.

ACKNOWLEDGMENT

Thank you to my son Scott and his family, son Mark, Ruth-Ann and her family, Nancy and her family, Rod and Kathy and their families. And Dad, woodsman, fisher, storyteller, you are my inspiration. You all hold up my world.

THE
KILLING JARS

KILLING JARS

Killing Jars come in various sizes and shapes, depending on their use. It is recommended to have 2 or more jars in the field, for insects of different types. Wide-mouthed jars are preferable to narrow-mouthed ones. Mason jars are easily obtainable. Several materials can be used as killing agents such as ethyl acetate and cyanide. Ethyl acetate is a much safer material to use than cyanide, but does not kill as quickly. Field specimens killed by ethyl acetate are usually more relaxed than those killed by cyanide, and less likely to be discolored...

Luke Trickett
UBC

chapter
ONE

Thunder cracked over the Cypress Hills like rifle shot, then a deep rumble, receding. Lightning licked the highest reaches of the lodge-pole pine forests illumined and hungry to lay its fire down on that prairie anomaly rising out of the short-grass and mustard like some geographical error. Straddling southern Saskatchewan and Alberta. Big hammerheads, dark and brooding and mauling. Sheets of rain spilled from the rent underbelly and drudged towards the dry June sections of the Trickett ranch. Windrush. And that gave a moment's respite to John Trickett as he pushed his coppered face up into the air fresh and clean and electric. The world turning in his blue eyes. Out for a walk after dinner along the same gravel track that scuffed the boots of his father. There at the margins of the ranch where the cottonwoods dispensed their seeds like slow snow and the soft drifts of it gathered in the spring ruts. A ranching fool who raised cattle and seed oil in an uncertain economy. American subsidies and Trickett soil blowing clear to Manitoba.

And his wife Nora, always aware of his moodiness, held his arm and his bearing as if to let go would see him run crazed and desperate into those hills that held up his world. Hair braided and a cotton blouse and the infinite wells of her grey eyes. An accountant who couldn't balance the ledger. But she knew her way around men and had taken up swearing as an equalizer. "It'll come, John," she said. "That cloud is one black son of a bitch." Squeezed his arm and ducked down to catch his troubled gaze.

"I smell it plain enough." He looked overhead, away from her, but the rain was stalled. It might not even fall. June teased a man, mocked with that throaty growl. Boulders tumbling in a stream. The blackbirds along Maple Creek were silenced by it and the barn swallows all but vanished. Conspiring against another generation of Tricketts who never had the good sense to quit the prairie. He stopped and lowered his head and stared at the ground. As if there lay the meaning of it all. But there was only the slick taper of coyote shit. Squatting in ridicule under the quartering moon.

"What's the matter, John?"

"Nothing."

"You won't talk to me, but you'll talk to Harley Buck."

"Harley understands things."

"So what do you want me to do, not say anything to you?"

"No."

"Then talk to me."

He stepped over the turd and tested the air with his nose and jammed his hands in his pockets. "I just have this feeling lately," he said. "Sadness. I can't shake it. I don't know what's wrong with me." He stopped again and turned to her bravely. Standing there in his ranch outfit. Jean jacket with a corduroy collar and jeans and a baseball hat with New Holland on the crown. White cotton shirt with western cut pockets. Watson gloves stuffed in his back pocket. Big hang-bum.

"Your mom and dad sick in town. And the boys off to university this fall. That's reason enough to be sad."

"Yeah."

"You don't seem so sure."

There was something else. A week before, he drove into the

Cypress Hills after a day on the tractor. To watch the sun go down. Grasses dancing in the cool breezes, swaying in brassy waves and aspen quaking, whispering all is well. His mind seemed suited for a view like that, looking out over Windrush shimmering on the heated table of the world and beyond the lamps of Maple Creek twinkling like the first stars. Old Cowtown. His contained life. Nothing else seemed to exist. And that was troublesome to John Trickett. He loved the rancher's life under that dome of endless blue days. But that was all he knew. Never been west of Medicine Hat or east of Regina. His life half over and his dreams all but quit him.

"I thought it would be different," he said. "I always figured things would turn out just the way I planned."

"Life doesn't give a shit about your plans, John."

"Dad never taught me otherwise. In fact, I don't think he was much help to growing boys. 'Just get out there and work til' you blister, Johnny,' he would say."

"That kind of talk will likely kill a man."

"Yeah, but I remember something else about him. When we finished high school, he seemed kind of relieved. He said, 'now's the time to dream.'"

"That's something."

"And I believed it. So did Luke. We worked out all the details of our dream. I was the oldest and would get the ranch house. We would build Mom and Dad a little place out back for their retirement. And Luke would have a place of his own. Just over there by the creek." He pointed to a rise in the land. A mountain blue bird on the fence wire tilting in the wind. The thrashing of grass beneath the cottonwoods and the dark sky like lead. The prairie stretching on and on.

"You know how many times you've pointed to that place?"

Ignored her or didn't hear. "We would run Windrush together. Raise our kids. One big happy family. But he's gone. Mom and Dad are dying and my sons don't want no part of this life."

"You're forgetting, John, they're my sons too."

"Yeah, I know it."

"They have their own dreams."

"And that's they way it should be. It don't make it any easier. Raising boys to men. Then to let them go. I never thought it would be this hard. Everything ending."

"You want to quit this place?"

"Do you?"

"I'm not ready to quit this life. Don't forget, I'm that Vancouver neophyte accountant you fell for on that hot as hell day in Regina when I took that summer job with the Cattlemen's Association. Didn't know the difference between bull shit and bullshit."

"I remember. You wondered where my cowboy hat was."

"You said you were wearing it. Maple Creek Golf Club."

"Never even golfed there. Harley gave me that cap. And I gave it to you."

"I wouldn't have found you without it. I owe Harley that much."

"No, I can't quit, Nora. Ranching is all I know. All I ever wanted to do. It's tough some times. The drought. Mad Cow and all that. And now without the boys to help."

"It'll be tough. Might have to hire someone."

"Yeah."

"If the rain comes, John, and we get a good yield. Put some weight on the stock. Windrush will pay this year. I'm sure of it." Said it for him.

They had walked far enough. They looked away from each other, always watching the land as if there might be something different there. Talking without looking into each other eyes. Studying the prairie for a clue that might console their worrying. Then the rain began to fall in a thin drizzle. Nora's cotton blouse became wet and stuck to her skin. And John turned to her and smiled and saw how the cool rain clung to her and how her nipples rose up. He turned away when she caught him looking. She poked him in the belly that hung over his belt.

"What were you looking at, John Trickett?"

"Nothing," he said. Said it a thousand times.

Then a impish grin and she took his hand and walked him to the grass that grew deep and soft near the creek. Beneath the cover of a cottonwood bending above them. The leaves inverted silver. "Take off your jacket, sweety" she said. Still smiling that rendered him useless and thick- headed. Didn't know what she was up to. Didn't want to stop her. Placed his jacket on the grass and flattened it as she peeled off her boots and jeans. Looked over her shoulder towards the house. Just the grey film of rain slanting there in the open.

"What's got into you?" he said. His jeans pooling around his ankles as he knelt down between her legs. Giggling like those prairie nights in 1975 when she found Maple Creek. Asked for John Trickett at the golf club.

"I just know what you need sometimes." She allowed her arms to fall to her sides.

He unbuttoned her blouse and stared down at her. So beautiful and real and growing old with him. Her belly was full and round and her thighs heavier than they used to be. He kissed her and she reached around his waist and pulled him into her.

"Not ready," he said. He felt awkward. Embarrassed in front of his wife. Something wasn't right. He lifted himself and peered over the grass. The prairie was still there. Water settled in the ruts along the track and a barn swallow set down and picked up a kernel of mud.

"It's alright," Nora said. A hand across her forehead.

"I don't think so," John said. "Broken down son of a bitch." Sat with his bare ass on his jacket and turned to his wife naked from her waist down. That familiar place and her legs angled obliquely for him.

She sat up and held him in her hand. The soft feel of her touch. Coaxing with silent rhythms. "There now," she said, "I have a place for that."

Nora fell backwards onto the grass and John felt his way into her. Not one to give up. His anxiety melted as his weight pressed her into the earth. The smell of love and new grass and the soft language of love rising and falling. Her breath in his ear and a truck coming along the track.

"Damn, it's the boys," John said, "get dressed." A little panicked.

"Shit, something's up," Nora said.

The truck pulled up. Skidded in the mud like grease. They jumped out of the truck as their parents emerged from the tall grass.

"What were you doing down there?" Del said.

"You're soaking wet," Mitch pointed out.

"Oh, just checking the level of the creek," John said. Looked away, then glanced down to check his fly. His shirt half tucked. He felt like a teenager caught at something unwholesome. He knew it wasn't, but still he had that guilty feeling. Those times too long in the bathroom and his father banging on the door calling out, 'what are you doing in there?'

"And how is it?" Del asked. He turned to his younger brother and shot out his elbow. Mitch's hand covered his mouth.

"Don't forget, you two," Nora said. "I'm the one who prepares your food. Now what the hell's the matter?" Always direct when it came to her boys. Or anything.

"It's Grandpa," Del said. "He called again. Third time tonight."

"Now what?" John said.

"He said Grandma is acting strange."

"Alzheimers will do that." He didn't mean to be insensitive in front of his sons. Frustrated to tears by his parent's situation that was growing worse by the day. He knew his mother ought to be in Swift Current where she could be cared for in a proper facility. But his father wouldn't have it. And with his lung cancer slowly killing him, he needed to be in a hospital himself. But they couldn't be together and he wasn't about to quit on her. She had been there for him all through the lean ranch years and never complained. No, he wouldn't leave her. Lived in a small rented house in Maple Creek with a patch of grass and a weedy garden. Would live there together until the end.

"He said she's been holding onto an old newspaper for two days and won't let go of it. He wants you to come over quick. He sounds really worried, Dad. She won't let Grandpa take it from her."

John's head sagged. All his troubles.

"You go on, John," Nora said. Kissed him on the cheek, then placed her arms around her sons for the walk back to the house.

The truck kicked up a bole of dust from beneath the thin film of mud and John Trickett looked out into the side mirror and watched his family shrink and the prairie boundless around him. The sun leaked through the breaking clouds and the cottonwoods ignited there along Maple Creek against the steel backdrop of Montana. The gullies were lost in shadow and the wan undulations rising lit and remote. Ford diesel gurgling. Sharp-tailed grouse rocketing. Thought of Nora there in the grass and sensed his father's duty.

chapter

TWO

The front door was unlocked and he found his father sitting in the living room in his favorite chair. He was hooked up to the oxygen bottle on the floor beside him, tubes stuffed in his nose like an alien newly arrived. It seemed that someone had let the air out of him. Wizened. Skin like the parched earth. His mother in a twin chair staring woodenly at the television and her hair disheveled and the buttons on her sweater misaligned and that newspaper clenched in thin hands. Knobs of knuckles erupting bony and white. She never looked up.

"See for yourself," Walter Trickett said. He gave his head a slight tilt.

"Have one of the nurses been in to see you, Dad?" John said. Looking around the room for some clue that they had. It put his mind at ease to have nurses visit his parents. They kept an eye on their health. It was poor health, but they were managing. It seemed that they might last the summer. The ranch took all his time. Still he came to town every second day. There was always something that needed to be done. Paying bills and buying groceries and asking a lot of questions. "Dad?"

"No."

"Are you getting around alright?" It looked like the room had been ransacked.

"Where the hell do you think I'm to go?" Cranky and every reason to be. False teeth on the coffee table. Grinned at a jar of peanut butter.

"You have to look after things, Dad. That's the deal."

"I'm looking after things. Don't get on me, John. Just watching the news."

"How's the pain today?"

"Like it is everyday." A grimace slashing his puckered mouth.

"Take your morphine?"

"It makes me constipated."

"No cigarettes?"

He looked away. "No smokes."

John went into the kitchen. Picking up as he went. "Has Mom been eating?" Opened the fridge door. The water jug was nearly full. Uneaten casseroles crusted stale and wasted.

"I can't get her to do anything. That's why I called. Look at the newspaper. She won't let go of it." Short sentences and shorter breaths.

"You have to keep your fluids up. Mom too."

"Yeah."

"You need to help Mom to the bathroom. Have you done that?"

"She won't let go of the newspaper."

Stomped into the living room. More fear than anger. "You got to look after her, Dad. If you don't, you know what I'll have to do. And I don't want to do it. I want to keep you together as long as possible. But I think that time is nearly over. We have to face it."

"I want to die here, John." Walter began to cry. A deep down sobbing that left him breathless. He raised his old banana finger and waved it in a circular motion. Above his head. Around and around. "She thinks it's Luke."

"Luke?" John said. His eyes closing. His great shoulders sagging. Sorry for his words that made his father cry. It didn't take much.

Never cried a day in his life. But now he cried over what seemed some little thing. Except there were no more little things in Walter Trickett's life.

"There's a likeness."

John knelt down in front of his mother. She looked past him. He tried to pry the newspaper from her claws. It began to tear.

"See what I mean?"

"Where did she get the paper?"

"Old Gerty Buck brought over some jam. Two year old jam. Can you believe it?"

"Come on, Dad, that was considerate of her. Can't you be grateful for once?"

"For what"

"Never mind." Shakes his head, but his father doesn't notice. Shakes his head at the long suffering.

"Stuffed in a box lined with that newspaper. She was alright then. A few days ago. She could look after herself pretty good. I'd help of course. Bathe her. Toilet her. Then she removed the jars of that old jam and there it was. Some story. A picture of a fella. And in the background. Well, it could be Luke. I doubt like hell it is. But Mother, here, she's convinced that she's found Luke. I don't know what to do about it, John. She's all froze up about it. I always thought it was the guilt that made her sick. All her life trying to forget him. She never could. Now that picture has brought it all back. Don't know what to do. Called you four times tonight. Finally got Del on the line. What were you doing?"

"Praying for rain. And you called three times, Dad."

"Three. I suppose. What the hell does it matter?" Bats at the dust motes held in a beam of sunlight. Galaxies swirling. Untouched by his frantic breaths.

"It doesn't. I'm here now. Calm down, Dad."

"What are you going to do, John?"

Leaned to catch his mother's idle stare. Nothing. He dropped his head thinking that he might have to call for a social worker to come for her. Sign the papers that were waiting. Put his father in the Maple Creek Hospital. Get it over with. His father would fuss. But it couldn't be helped. It made him sick in his stomach to think about separating them. Against his father's will. There was no denying the end of one's life and the pain and grief that would surely follow. But there was grief in witnessing a slow death, something more despairing to look upon the racked and ravaged body of a strong man. That weathered old cowboy who smoked two packs a day since the war. And the ebb and close of a mother's life.

Desperately. A boy's whisper. "You have a picture of Luke, Mom?"

Something unhinged. Her mouth began to open. Still her eyes fixated on the television. Some other channel.

"Can I see?" He slowly let his hand rest on his mother's unyielding grip. Patted it.

Then her eyes left the television and she looked right at him. Her son. Returned to the world of the living. Eyes brimming with tears that ran down the creases of her face. The salted river beds of her life. She let go of the paper and John took it and smoothed the folds over his knee. Palmed the pages. There was only one section of the paper. A Toronto daily. The title of the article: *The Lost Ones. A Story of Fringe-Dwellers Living in the Ravines of Toronto.* The homeless hidden away in the carved out river bottom amidst the bustle of millions. There were photos of the residents. A young man with his toque pulled down. Hair sprouting and listless eyes vaguely aware. And behind him in the distance someone turning away from the camera. Caught in mid-step escaping. A hand coming up to conceal. The caption read: *Steven panhandles for spare change while the Bug Man collects insects in jars. 'He's a freak,' Steven says.* The word Bug Man was circled with a pen.

A chill set down upon John Trickett, a rush of air like someone passing. Cool across his cheek. He turned to his father and remembered Luke's letter that revealed the first symptoms, the signs of delusion. His mother's gasp. Sickness in the family on her side, hidden away and nonexistent. Emerging in her own family. Her second son.

"Did Mom write on this paper, Dad?"

"No, I doubt it. I won't let her have a pen, John. Might stab herself or something."

"Dad, where are Luke's things?" John said. Seized now by what his mother knew.

"A box in the closet. In the bedroom. What there is of it. It's all there, John. What are you thinking?"

He went to the bedroom and pulled a cardboard box from the closet and carried it back into the living room. He sat on the floor and rummaged through it, sifting, sorting through Luke's life. Report cards and pictures he drew in elementary school. Christmas ornaments that didn't make the tree. Hockey team photos. A little album secreted away. Just a boy. A normal life on a ranch. On the back written in pencil: *Johnny and Luke, Christmas 1965.* Every picture of Luke in the box. His life stricken from the earth. A blue ribbon for a prize bull. An envelope post marked February 1979 that read: *Tricketts, Maple Creek.*

> *Dad, Mom and Johnny*
> *The life of bugs. It is no wonder I like it. Jars of things that seem dead. Floating. Watching me. Trying to get out. I told the Prof. and he said that they are all dead. Who killed them for me to look at? Someone said that I should let them out. In my head. Try telling me that I shouldn't. Goddamn them. Next time you go turn out the porch light, see the moths I let out. See them come to crawl on me in the dorm when the lights go out and the dumb fucks don't believe me. Those dumb fucks want to steal my killing jars. But they won't find them. Look at the porch light.*

Little pills like larvae, I won't take them.
Luke
UBC Department of Entomology

"What is it, John?" Walter Trickett said.

"It might be him," he said gravely. The implication.

"Luke? It's been nearly twenty five years."

"I think he's the Bug Man."

"There's a likeness."

John Trickett folded the letter and returned the envelope to the stack of papers and pulled out a sheet yellowed and musty. It was from Luke's doctor. Said Luke had Paranoid Schizophrenia and was hospitalized. He was receiving medication and would soon be able to return to Maple Creek under a doctor's care and his family's support. He didn't get either.

A fourth year student. It all ended. The dream ended. Luke was to have his degree in Entomology and bring home a new way of farming and ranching. No more pesticides. Luke and John both had been affected by *Silent Spring* by Rachel Carson. It was their plan to introduce natural insects to carry out pest control. Organic farming was the way of the future. An environmental friendly operation. Luke never finished his final term. First his letter came and then the doctor's letter. Luke did return to Maple Creek, but John Trickett's best friend never arrived. Someone else took his place.

Sitting there in the grim light of dusk he pushed the box away and sat in silence. His father rasping away. A mouth breather. His mother listening to the unspoken words of the past. His mind drifting back to that summer night on Jasper Street. They had all come to town for a rare dinner out. Nora had met Luke the previous summer. Some saint among the Tricketts. She knew how John loved him and how they would beat that thing, together, as if it were something that could be overcome. Willed to the netherworld.

Then not a minute out of the truck, Luke spotted a family of tourists all wearing matching sweatshirts with a dragonfly pattern gilded sparkling and bright. He nearly ripped the clothing off their backs to get at the dragonflies and had to be handcuffed by an RCMP constable who had just finished his dinner at the 2 Cool 4 U Cafe. Children crying and parents screaming. John's mother collapsed there in the street. He remembered it all. And his mother and father committing Luke to an institution in Vancouver. Some hellish old place in the Fraser Valley. A view through steel bars.

"What are you going to do, John?"

"Why didn't we visit him?"

"We did visit him. But you had to stay with the ranch."

"Just that once."

"He never knew us. Or he didn't want to. Upset to be there. I don't know. But your mother could never go back. Had to let it all go. We all did. He didn't know us, John. He had a sickness that wasn't going to get better."

John Trickett turned to his mother sitting. Her eyes cast downward. Her chest moving slightly with her shallow breath pulling slightly on the misaligned button on her sweater. He reached over to her and made it proper. Looked around the room that was cluttered with life's attainment. The stuff of flea markets. "She made us forget him. Over and over. I had a family of my own. I listened to her."

"It was for the best."

"How could she just let him go. Her son. My brother?" He paid no mind to his mother's acuity. He assumed she had none. Just that insipid gazing.

Air leaking out his black hole. Past his shriveled gums. "It was in her family. Schizophrenia."

"I know that. Her older brother. Died of pneumonia."

"No. That's what she told you."

"How then?"

"It happened in the winter. It was her mother that had pneumonia. Real sick. Her father had to take her to the hospital. They lived on a farm near Saskatoon. Her father took the other children with him and left your mother with your uncle Tommy. In the spring they were to take him for electric shock treatments. She was only fourteen, but she was a capable girl. Just sit with him until they got back. Well, a bad storm kept her father in Saskatoon. He called and said he would send a neighbour, but she said she was alright. Things were quiet. Nothing unusual. She made sure he got to bed before she turned in herself.

"In the morning she found him hanging from a beam in the kitchen. Blue dead. Hanging like a chandelier. Poor child couldn't do anything. The storm was raging. The phones went out. She sat there in the kitchen staring up at him for two days before the weather cleared and the Mounties came at the calling of her father. Two days in that kitchen with her dead brother. The smell of him. She thought that was going to happen to Luke. Find him hanging in the morning. It was her greatest fear. A suffocating fear. The hospital was the safest place for him. Until they closed the damn place and he fell through the cracks. He lived in a Group Home. He walked away one day. And that was that. Fell through the cracks. Bastards!"

"She's lived with that nearly her entire life," John said taking his mother's cold hands and cupping them in his own. Like chilled sausage links. Could she understand? He turned to his father. Worn out. Slow eyed and used up.

"She understands," Walter said. "Don't you, Mother?" Leaned over to show his son.

They both looked at her. Her chin trembling. Crumpling, and her eyes boiling over. Then she leaned forward in her chair and raised her shivering hand. Pointed to the window. A flutter of chalk white wings and antennae like ferns. Tapping. Tapping. "Bring him home, Johnny," she said. A thin quail's voice. "Bring Luke home. Promise me."

chapter
THREE

Harley Buck could see John Trickett coming from way back at his barns. Windrush was on the opposite side of Highway 21 and the long gravel driveway came out at the same spot. That rising dust following. So Harley always knew when John went into town. He would gauge his business and loaf out near the highway until he came back. He would fiddle with an irrigation pipe. Fence post. Dead prairie dog. If there was nothing handy he would pop the hood on his truck. John Trickett was going to stop anyway. He always did.

He pulled into Harley's driveway and turned off the ignition and waited for Harley to see him there. After a time he looked up. Faked being surprised to see him. Couldn't hear the diesel complaining or the crunch of gravel under the wheels. Checking the oil out at the highway.

"Hey, John, hot enough for you?" Harley said. He had a head of snow white bristles under his straw cowboy hat that he was prone to scratch. Feverish in the summer heat. His shoulders were always well flaked from such habits. A man lean and sharp featured. A chaw tucked behind his lip and watery blue eyes.

John walked over to Harley's truck and leaned over a fender. Looking haggard. "I don't mind the heat," he said. Took off his cap and wiped his forehead with the back of his hand. "It's the cows that don't like it."

Harley nodded in agreement. The prairie lamented some tune through the telephone wires. That sad old song of drought and piss poor prices. Harley looked up to acknowledge the sentiment. The blue sky and the moon just a scrape of chalk and a pair of mourning doves rising up from the ditches. "How's your folks, John?"

"They're getting by. A nurse spends most of the day with them now."

"Did they get that jam Gerty sent over?"

That old jam. Flushed with guilt over his father's comment. "Yeah, I appreciate that. Tell Gerty I said so."

"Damn shame to see old Walter like that. We grew up together. Me and your dad."

"I know that, Harley."

"Smoked like a chimney."

"Yeah." John Trickett stepped back from Harley's truck. Looked around as if it mattered. Down the highway and over to Windrush. He could make out Del and Mitch blurred in the heat waves by the barns. A world through cellophane. Nora somewhere. "What do you know about Toronto, Harley?"

Harley tipped the brim of his straw hat and scratched his stubby forelock to consider the question.. A loop of tobacco juice tumbling."My sister Irene went out with Johnny Bower."

"I'm not talking about a hockey team, Harley."

"Then I don't know a damn thing, John."

"But you read the paper."

"Don't have time for papers." Started to reach for his cowboy hat.

"There was a section from one of those city papers in that box of jam."

"Yeah, I suppose there might have been."

"I was wondering if you might have circled part of an article with a pen. Just a word."

"What the hell are you talking about, John?"

"I need to know. It's important."

"Hell, I got that paper from Nora." Harley stood back and eyed John, perplexed, the dipstick in his hand dripping on the gravel in black gobs. "At a cattlemen's meeting. You know Nora. She wanted me to read an article on foot-and-mouth disease. Said we should think about diversifying. You remember that. The cat calls and such. She said we should look at natural gas exploration. Historical and eco-tourism. Whatever the hell that is. Said that we're putting too much emphasis on hamburgers. Beef promotions should include a healthy lifestyle. Hell, those boys were ranchers. Thought she was off her nut. She tried to make a fool out of me, John."

"You oughtn't have said what you did, Harley. Not to Nora."

"Damn John, she asked me to rise. Wanted to know what I thought about manure management. Putting me on the spot. I knew it. I said, 'how the hell should I know, I didn't vote Liberal.' Well , I never thought the boys would laugh so hard. How was I to know. In fact some the old timers pissed themselves. One of my finest moments, by God."

"Nora's not stupid, Harley." John looked down at the mess Harley was making. A fool thing to do. He had a garage and all the tools. A paper towel dispenser. And yet he waited out at the highway just so he could gab. He would never call on the telephone. Never go for a cup of coffee in Maple Creek. He waited out at the highway with the hood of his truck popped. The doctor is in. Thought he was a cowboy shrink. Leased most of his land and ran a few head of cattle. Two old horses that escaped from the glue factory.

"I never called her stupid, John. Hell, I know she's got her degree and all that. Smart as a whip about figures. Knows more about ranch management than any of us. But some of the boys, well, you know. She's a woman. And they're not used to listening to a woman unless they're being called to supper."

"And I thought you had an open mind, Harley."

"Open enough to know my place in the world. Bucks aren't farmers. My great granddad Orville Buck was one of the first policemen in this country. After he left the service he worked cattle on these same stubby plains. What the hell do we know about seed oil?" Spat like a fouled cherub. "No offense, John. I admire Nora. I know she don't care for my point of view. But this business depends a lot on hamburgers. Fat kids or not. Can't blame that on ranchers."

"We've had our moments, Harley. Don't think that we haven't. But one thing I've learned about Nora, is that she looks ahead. Looks into the future. Tries to see where all this is going. I think it is a good thing. She convinced me to put in that canola. It was her idea. It was a money maker."

"Yeah, and she held Windrush together as I recall, John. I know what she means to you. Some men need a strong woman like that."

"What the hell do you mean, some men?" John Trickett's button.

"Now, John, don't get all fussed. We all loved Luke. But we were all worried about you. It could have happened to any man. She nursed you back from your grieving. Your mom and dad will never forget it. I'm grateful myself."

He hung his head remembering. Stared between his boots. That anxious feeling in his belly planted there by a thought. As if its formlessness manifested into a sickly wad of something. "You wouldn't have had anyone to talk to, Harley," he managed.

"I suppose, but I'm a good listener too." Harley's old dog lumbered down the long driveway and parked in the shade of his truck. Tired of waiting. A short haired porch sitter.

"I know it."

"Does Nora still think I'm corrupting you?"

"Something like that."

"A man needs a man to talk to sometimes. Old Nug here would as soon sleep as listen to my babble." Reached down and rubbed an ear until Nug's head flopped over. Asleep.

"She can't figure out why I confide in you, that's all. Two grown men leaning over a fender. Why don't you check the oil back at the barns?"

"Would you have stopped to tell me all your troubles?"

"I asked you what you knew about Toronto."

"I don't know a damn thing about Toronto. Just Johnny Bower. What's going on, John?"

John Trickett walked over to his truck and reached through the window and grabbed the newspaper article and returned to Harley leaning over the gravel with his nose pinched between his thumb and index finger blowing his snot. Ropes of it hanging. Cleaned up with a sleeve. Seemed to refresh him. Nug unimpressed.

"Who does that look like?" John said tapping the photo with his finger. Their eyes met like strangers.

"That there?" Harley looked down through his nose. Reared his head back. He took his reading glasses from his shirt pocket and put them on and stuck his face in and out like a see-saw. "Behind that scruffy bugger."

"Yeah, I see him. Looks like Luke. Son of a bitch, John. That scrawny bastard looks like Luke. That what's your thinking, isn't it? Luke all skinny and middle-aged."

"It could be."

"You think you've found him." He looked out over the prairie as if it were something sentient embodied in the dried out skin of summer. Eavesdropping on misguided plans. The shrill of the mocking wires.

"I don't know, Harley. It could be Luke. It seems someone else thinks so too." Points to the blue swirl around, *Bug Man*.

"Not me, John. And it wasn't Gerty. She wouldn't know Luke from a fence post."

"Curious, don't you think?"

"You'll need to speak to your better half, my friend. Leave me the hell out of it."

"I'm kind of worried about that."

"If you're thinking of going to Toronto to find him, you better tell Nora that it was all your idea. I'll never hear the end of it."

"I know it, Harley."

"She helped you forget him. Don't you forget that."

"I never forgot him. And Harley, I promised my mother I would bring Luke home."

"Now that is serious. Promises and such. Still, Nora won't like it, John. Good God of Mercy, she won't like it one bit. You best be sure about this. Write a letter to someone in Toronto. The newspaper. See what you can find out before you go off half-cocked."

John Trickett nodded. Harley made sense a good part of the time. A man sprouted from the earth was well weathered and wise. Rarely went indoors except to eat. He knew the prairie and all its offerings. Always something to forecast the future. And the future gathered along the fences and tracked across the roof of the world where he read it like the clouded parchment of the almanacs. Harley Buck was a loyal friend. A plain and simple man of singular ambition.

Harley shoved the dip-stick back in the tube made for it and slammed the hood shut and dusted off his cracked and leathered hands like clapping the dust out of a pair of time-worn gloves. "I knew you were troubled, John," Harley said. "I had a feeling."

"Troubled?"

"You know. Men tend to sulk and women tend to cry. You won't believe this, but I would rather see a man cry and get back in the barns to do a days work than a sulker not worth a damn for a week."

"I'm not sulking."

"I know you're not. Just sad as you've always been over Luke." Pawed the air.

"I don't think on it directly. But it's there. I'll admit that."

"When we lost old Nug's mother, I was sad some."

"You're comparing losing Luke to losing an old dog?"

"Geez, John. No. Everyone thinks that it's either this way or that. Black or white. But things aren't like that. Hell, when old Charlie Triphammer passed away, I wasn't that sad about it. But his family grieved a great deal. Just depends on how close a man is to the fire. Old Walter seemed to accept losing Luke. Your mother, well, no one grieves like a mother. And I know you and Luke were close. I understand how you hurt. Probably never get over it."

"Do you think I'm a fool to want to find him?"

"You'll never be a fool if what speaks to you is in your belly. That's a deep down thing. Sometimes sadness is just something trying to get your attention. Something that needs looking at. Perhaps something that needs to be resolved once and for all. Still, it might not work out. That's a possibility, John. You won't be able to predict what you may find."

"I think I have to try."

"I'd never convince you otherwise." Spat a muddy slurry.

"A man my age living in a small world. In all this space. It makes me feel a little shaky. To know that there is a world out there unknown to me."

"That don't mean shit, John. Hell, I haven't been nowhere myself. Just ranching. What it means is that I know the ground below my feet better than any man. Know my home and my place. This is the spot God gave me. I'll never be sorry for it. Grateful for this life."

John nodded. "What do I owe you, Doc?"

"Not a damn thing. I owe you for putting up with me. This short grass prairie gets lonesome at times. Gerty can't hear that well. And you're the only one that'll listen to me. I aim to be helpful. Raised beef all my life. Spent most of it in the company of those bovines. Never cared to talk to them. You're not a judging man, John. I can talk to a man like that."

John Trickett looked off into the distance as was the habit of ranchers. His eyes pinched against the glare of the sun. Mindful that the prairie did not stop at the pearl horizon of gathered clouds that seemed to have fallen weighty from the sky. He projected his notion of the infinite upon such far seeing. His world upon the terrestrial sea. The prairie had an end and something lay beyond. Something unaffected by his musings. Things that Harley said. And things unspoken. The unfolding of life in all its strange tapestries that could not be contrived by sobered imagination. And he knew well enough that another world lived in the minds of some. Something of hellish fantasy. A nightmarish world, abstract confusion. There in the ravines of Toronto.

chapter
FOUR

The dining room in the Trickett ranch house was made for the labouring times fifty odd years gone when Windrush required the efforts of a dozen men with the will to create a life in the short-grass. Men happy to heap spuds like thunderheads alongside slabs of beef on their noon plates. That family of toilers now reduced to the mechanized few. The seasonal help of comers and goers. Now just the Tricketts. Dwindling. Del and Mitch embracing the new age of universality. The global village. Gone in less than two months.

The silence of Sunday dinners. As if the awkwardness of speech might leak those guarded truths of a family teetering on the precipice of disassociation. Not that truth was not welcome in the Trickett home. Nora's virtue. But the fear of endings smashed the hope and possibilities of new beginnings. Nora watched her boys and at once seeing the empty chairs. The empty house. Creaking floors and the wind in the eaves mournful, howling like a chained dog. And John saw it in her eyes. The fear of losing her boys to the jaws of perdition. That a voice may steal upon them and whisper its madness. The haunting background music in her brain. And the Bug Man stuffed in his back pocket.

"Spent a lot of time with Harley this afternoon," Nora said. "What's the old bandit spinning today?"

"Oh you know, the same old things." Eyes flitting over his plate. "That's all? You were there a while."

Could feel her hot welds. "He was just wondering about Mom and Dad."

Del and Mitch like redwoods. Big boys who had outgrown their father by a half a foot. Watched the slow burn.

John Trickett turned to his sons. Couldn't look at Nora. Couldn't take the newspaper from his pocket. "Go see your grandparents. When you get a chance. It will do them good. Pick up their spirits." They both nodded that they would.

The image of Luke. Felt it pleading. His heart fluttering. Anxiety visiting, demanding action or death. He reached for the article and pulled it out already folded neat and ready with that picture, that likeness and blue ink circling. He placed it down on the table beside the peas like a napkin and Del and Mitch watched him with curious indifference and Nora put down her fork and rested her chin in the cup of her hand. She looked down at it as if it were a summons to some heinous crime. She turned away with her eyes closing. The clock on the mantle in the living room. Tick. Tick.

"Boys," John Trickett said watching Nora, "I got that new battery for the big Ford today. How about installing it. When you're finished."

Fast eaters. They wiped their mouths and pushed back on the table. They guessed the topic that coiled like smoke between their parents. They had seen it before. Wisps of it that never amounted to much. Those silent and partitioned evenings. Now there was a thickening between them. Chair legs dragging across the hardwood floor as they excused themselves. A brace of discordant trumpets.

A housefly lit upon the light fixture over the table. Never just a common thing. Beak. Maxillary palp. Sucking mouth parts. Waited for the door to close shut. "You knew that it was Luke," John said evenly. Still that word split like a wedge through seasoned wood. Dividing. Wounding knotted souls. He let his fingers slide across the newspaper, stretching to touch her.

She turned back to him as his fingertips hesitated. Withdrew. Face flushed before him. The return of the irreconcilable. His offering of tenderness and understanding. "I knew that face," she said.

"Why didn't you tell me about it?"

"Because I knew you would have that look that I see right now."

"What look is that?"

She closed her eyes and drew her breath deep down into her belly. Grappling with her honesty. "I feel like I'm losing you," she said. "A little more every day."

"It's more than that."

"That's not enough?"

"It's the boys."

"Yes, the boys. I fear for them. Not a waking moment. And now you want to find him. Tell me it is not true. Tell me you weren't talking to Harley about him. Never to me."

"I can't talk to you about Luke."

"Because he makes what I fear, real. Don't you see, John. God!"

"Nora, I failed him more than anyone. Left him for dead. I can't pretend that he doesn't exist. You can't ask me to do that. Not any more."

"Just let him go, John." Rose from her chair knocking it over. "Fuck you!" she said to it. Swung at it and kicked at it. Stormed into the kitchen and muttered and fumed and banged the cupboards.

John picked up the chair and followed her. She stood at the sink with her arms held stiffly over it. Her head down. Sobbing. Apple pie on a wire rack. Coffee warming. Accouterments of an ordered life.

"I'm going to find him," John said. No asserting tone to sway her.

Nothing. She took the apron hanging by the sink and dried her cheeks. Watching Del and Mitch at the big doors. They looked back at the house as they worked. Their stiff worried mouths. Fledgling barn swallows shouldering on the telephone line like Christmas lights. The prairie gaping beyond the barn.

"What, you're just going to get in your truck and drive to Toronto?" Tearful laughter. Disbelieving. John had always been predictable. Had a routine like a good dog. She just fed him and pointed him towards the barns and the prairie. Out you go now. Be back for dinner. That simple man that she loved. Counted on his unswerving commitment to Windrush. To her.

"Yeah, I suppose."

"Do you have a clue where you're going?"

"No."

"You've never been off the prairie."

"I've been thinking about that."

"You'll get lost."

"I'm already lost."

"They're leaving, John." She turned to face him. "Don't you want to spend time with them?" She tilted her head wearily to serve with the inflection in her voice rising, dripping with guilt. Good with coffee and pie.

"Yeah. I'll be back. There'll be time."

"And your mom and dad?"

"I know."

"It's no time to leave."

"If I don't go and find Luke now, I'm not going to be worth a damn to anyone. I feel like I'm cracking inside. Like something's going to bust."

"What?"

"I don't know. Rage. It just seems that nothing else matters more than this, Nora. I'm scared as hell, but still it feels right somehow."

"She was holding that paper in her hand."

"Yeah."

"You feel responsible now, to find him?"

"Something like that. I promised her."

"She's sick, John."

"Not when she said it. And it's just not that. There's more to it."

"Don't bring him back to Windrush."

"What?"

"This is no place for him."

"What, you're afraid the boys will catch something. Is that it?"

"I'll never forget that night in town when he attacked those girls. It was awful."

"He didn't attack them. He was confused. He was sick. It was his illness, Nora."

"He was crazy. The police came. I remember."

"We're all in this, don't you see? We owe Luke his life back."

"What life?"

"I don't know. I don't have the answers. Something."

"You can't bring him back, John. Tell me you won't."

"You can't mean that, Nora. He's my brother." He saw something ugly flash across her cheeks. Down turned mouth quivering. Chin crumpling like tin foil. Wild alien eyes.

"I couldn't handle it. I'm sorry." She turned her back to him and folded her arms. Defiant.

"All this time, you've been glad that he's gone?" A revelation. "Son of a bitch." He turned away with his hands raised as if he were holding a bundle of planking. His mouth open like a dumb-ass.

She jerked around and took hold of his shoulder to turn him back. She never lied to him before. Kept her feelings to herself and shored him up when he needed it. She was the heart and soul of Windrush. Fought for a profit there in the dry stubble and could see pay dirt in natural gas. Sparked envy in every cowboy in the district save for Harley Buck. Her good looks and ranch savvy. "Yes," she said.

chapter
FIVE

He left them standing there conflicted and abandoned like a family seeing a father off to war. Never to be seen again. Lost to something looming in the east that waited slavering and smacking its rude urban lips. The prime cuts of John Trickett all tender and chaste. Ignorant of the ways of the world that lay beyond the mustard vats pooling along the roadside like sulphur lakes where myriads of butterflies flitted about the waving blooms. Cabbage Whites like ping pong balls. Vastness stretching away from him in every direction. Dust dogs stirring along the margins. It seemed a comfort to him just then. Manageable images with their seasonal variation.

He hesitated at the end of his driveway thinking about such familiarity. Known things. He probed a canker in his mouth that was bothersome. Searched it out with his tongue and looked at it in the rearview mirror. A milky saucer that stung him fiercely. He looked down where the highway swept away the dusted arcs of his coming and going and then to Harley leaning on the fender of his truck scratching his festered scalp. The heat of the morning sun was not yet disagreeable. The glint of it white and glaring on his windshield. Nug asleep at his feet.

He looked up at a picture of Luke pinned to the sun-visor. He left his truck and walked across the highway. Looked both ways.

Thought a car went by the day before. Could feel the wind trying to lift his ball cap. It read Maple Creek Wheat Pool. A new hat for his trip. Held on to the brim. "I knew you'd be here," John Trickett said. He bent down on one knee and took a handful of loose skin that draped about Nug's neck. Gave a good rub. Nug shot out a leg to expose his underbelly and purple balls. Looked culpable.

"Hey, cut that out, Nug," Harley said. "Where's your manners?"

"Takes after the old man," John said.

Harley turned his head and cuffed the space between them. Swatting at a fly. Grinned until his chaw showed like a hedge against a picket fence. Seemed to like the remark just fine. "Yeah, I suppose he does," he said, "but you didn't stop to talk about Nug's pecker."

John pushed down on his knee and stood up and took a deep breath. He had the jitters. "No Harley, I didn't." He looked around as if there might be a prop handy that could explain the heaviness in his chest. Anxious as a virgin. Just thistle and a pop can and the bleached bones of something long dead. Bits of hide. All things returning to the earth.

"You're on your way, aren't you?"

"Yeah, on my way." Strain about his eyes. That sleepless look. He had turned in his bed and noticed Nora looking at the ceiling in the early hours. Couldn't bear to speak to her at breakfast with the tension syrup thick. Talked to the boys about feed schedules and confidence. Sitting there with his trembling hands under the table. Felt weak and inept but carried on.

"How did she take it?"

"Not well at all, Harley."

"She didn't think I had anything to do with it, did she?"

"She has her own opinions. You know that."

"Hell, I know, John. It's not a fault."

They both knew Nora would be watching from the porch. Watching their scheming. But it wasn't scheming to John Trickett. He was dead serious about his undertaking even if he was sick about it. He couldn't think beyond Maple Creek. His mind never had a context of things outside the view of the Cypress Hills. Couldn't imagine a city of millions. He just knew that he was about to get back in his pickup truck and leave. He turned to look at it. Like a fine horse that he could count on. A comfort on a long journey. Windrush painted on the door and ranch dust like a coffee stain above the running boards and the plug from the block heater dangling over Saskatchewan plates. Climb aboard and gallop off into the wilderness. But first he needed a favour from Harley.

"I need you to look in on the boys, Harley," he said earnestly. "Keep an eye on Windrush for me. I need you to do that. Likely I would take to worrying real bad and not be able to find Luke. Get flustered. If I knew you would be looking in on things, I would feel a lot better about this notion of mine. I would be grateful for it. More than you know. And I would like you to see how Nora's making out. Just ask her. You don't have to say more than that. Don't get into a conversation that might go sideways. Stay away from everything except the weather. You should be safe with that. But if she takes a different opinion, Harley, well just nod. You don't have to agree. I'm not telling you that. Sometimes a nod is just easier, that's all." He said it all at once without a breath or a pause so Harley wouldn't have time to interject, spit, paw the air, farmer blow or swallow his chaw.

"Hell, John, I had no idea you knew that many words."

"Does that mean you'll do it?"

"I'm not afraid of Nora. Glory be. Petrified's more like it." Straight faced.

"You're shittin' me, Harley."

"Geez, John, don't get all serious about this." Walked away from his truck chuckling and snorting. Astounded at such gullibility. Never understood how it concealed his real fear of Nora Trickett. "Of course I'll look in on your family. Your mother and father too. Don't you worry at all. I'm a cowboy by God."

"Thanks, Harley." Sucked at his canker and winced.

"Well." Harley nodded. "Did you make that phone call?"

"Yeah. I have to call this girl when I get into Toronto. A reporter. Said she would take me there. Where she wrote the article. She hadn't been back since." His voice cracking at the mere utterance of it.

"Well, I hope you find him, John. I hope you find your brother." Tugged on the brim of his cowboy hat to shade his watery eyes.

They stood mutely as the morning waned and the heat waves began to set the highway to wobble among the distant undulations. John looked over his shoulder to Windrush. Separation anxiety and he hadn't gone anywhere. Just a short distance outside Maple Creek in his mind. Then Nug stood up and staggered to the back of Harley's truck and pissed on his tire then ambled on towards the house and John Trickett took his leave.

chapter
SIX

He pulled off Highway 21 into Maple Creek and stopped in front of his parent's house and watched a nurse standing on the porch with her hands on her hips engaged in some talk with his father who stood with his mouth agape and his housecoat open exposing his wattled sack hanging grotesquely below his withered hips. She helped him cover up then pushed her way into the black cavern of infirmity. John Trickett had no stomach for a visit. Felt bad for thinking so. He worried that he might lose his nerve for the long drive to Toronto. Succumb to guilt. Grieve with regret.

He drove up Jasper Street and passed through town. There were those who left the modest shops and mercantiles and gathered on the street behind him to bear witness to such a spectacle. Men standing straddle-legged. As if some marvel manifested there before them. Some event of merit suited for the front page or a grandfather's knee. John Trickett, a pilgrim among them, setting out for the far reaches of the world. A pickup truck and rancher clad to save the Bug Man.

He turned east onto the Trans-Canada Highway. In Saskatchewan it was known for its straight stretches, as true and constant as the life that he was born in to. Just driving through the open expanse of prairie, unencumbered by chores and responsibilities. Through those small towns where everyone seemed a brother in that same jean outfit. Clones gabbing by their pickup trucks. They wore ball caps that read John Deere and Wheat Pools of every hick town and hamlet. Home Hardware. All manner of feedlots and video stores. Prince Albert Raiders in green and yellow. Swift Current Broncos. CN, CP, Petro-Canada, Remington, Husky, CAT, Finning and Ford. In every condition, faded, braided and bent to particularity. Sweat stained. Could stop and talk to any one of them over pie and coffee to consider the virtues of Herefords and Black Angus or Belgian Blues. Console a man who turned a failed crop back into the cracked and forsaken earth. Something that could happen to any one of them. Men like Harley Buck. Wise to the ways of the unforgiving prairie that gave life and took it back without so much as an apology. Never a good year to follow a bad one. A fraternity of stubborn stiff-gaited bastards who wouldn't quit on anything but would park their tractors and drive all day to Regina to cheer on the Roughriders.

On to Swift Current and Rush Lake. Prairie dogs and their daring dashes. Headlong and twitching on the roadside. And the flattened skins of the oblivious pressed into the macadam that was troublesome for coyotes and crows who equally paid the price for such carnage. And Ducks Unlimited potholes where all the water in Saskatchewan seemed to gather and the coots pleased and plentiful jerked their necks as they paddled back and forth as if they were looking for something lost to them. Barn swallows following along the highway margins as if those same fledglings sprung from the eaves of Windrush to keep him company. And they did just that until he reached Regina popping out of the prairie dressed in the accouterments of a city. Business towers with corporate logos, the dome of the world caught in an endless movie of blue sky in those high glass cubes that inferred vitality, but defied the farm economy.

Then there beyond Regina, at the cusp of everything known and unknown, the frontier lay before him, fresh and new and possible. A man could think in that kind of freedom. But John Trickett's mind did not align with such liberty. Pushing through the outer reaches of his comfort zone, his mind began to wander away from the benign landscape. He could feel the anxiety stewing in his belly. The pressure of his belt buckle against his stomach. The discomfort. Clammy hands. And then his mind went to Nora, compelled by some force of reckoning, what she said about Luke. What she didn't say. She was glad that Luke was gone and that changed everything. Skewed his perception. Altered what he believed about her. His wife of all those years holding back such secret thoughts. Harboured such resentment. It made his heart beat faster. Just the thought of it. And then his mind seemed to act on its own and began a stampede to conspire against her. Gathering old slights and annoyances and feeding them. He could taste the bitterness of blame on his lips. He gripped the steering wheel like a dentist's chair. Then a town appeared ahead of him. Prosper. He drove on through looking for a coffee shop. A cup of sanity.

He turned into a cafe at the outskirts. Towns like Propser had nothing to tempt him. A lifeless place with dust dogs working the streets and a few old-timers watching from the store fronts as if they had a question for him. What the hell is the point of all this? He stepped out of his truck and at once felt the heat. Everything glaring in Prosper. Named by a fool optimist, he estimated. Squinted and pulled his ball cap down. Some crop lay wasting behind the cafe. Grasshoppers wouldn't care for such a spindly yield. He felt bad for the poor bastard farmer who sweated his guts out over it.

He could smell fat cooking. Patty's Cafe. A sign tilting, cracked white of summers gone. One other car in the parking lot and an orange cat sitting in the shade of half dead tree licking the pink feet of a mole. The feet moved. John thought the ways of cats was cruel, playing with life and death like that. Thought the cat should kill it, put the little thing out of its misery. The zoom of Kenworths and Freightliners behind him as he went inside. The door was open, held by a brick.

He stood at the counter by the till and noticed an old woman scurrying around in the kitchen. Just a little thing in a grease stained apron. Mouse-like. A mop of white haired curls. Peeling potatoes, loading the sink with dirty dishes, putting clean ones away. Some meat sizzling on the grill. Salisbury steak. Onions spitting. Coiled flypaper hung above her head like filmstrip. A ceaseless worker; she never looked up. He stood there watching her, expecting a waitress to attend to him. He turned around and a middle-aged couple sat in a booth looking past one another. No words. All was quiet save for the buzz of flies and the industry of the old woman. He turned back and she was dropping handfuls of french fries into boiling fat, checked the salisbury steak and stirred the onions.

John dropped his keys on the counter. They made a sharp crack that startled him as it was not in his character to be so bold. She looked up at him, froze like a coyote just aware of an intruder. Someone watching.

"Are you all by yourself?" he said.

She stepped out from the kitchen drying her raw hands on her apron. Bone with the flesh burnt away. Blood smears on the apron. "Do you see anybody else back here?" A voice shouting and a little snippy.

"I just thought…"

"Well, what do you want? I don't have all day." Stood there with her bottom lip pushed up over her top lip like a bull dog. Her eyes squeezed together. The milky eyes of a woman half crazed. A look for his assumptions.

"Just a coffee."

"I ain't going to get rich on a coffee for God's sake." Tossed her hand up. "I got a special on. Salisbury steak and onions. French fries and coffee. $6.95. Didn't you see the sign outside?"

John looked over his shoulder and the middle-aged couple were both turned watching them. Afternoon entertainment. He wondered if it came with the special. Didn't see a sign. "I didn't see the sign," he said.

"Glory be. Outside, I said. Not in here. I put the sign outside to draw customers. Now what will it be, a special?"

He looked around the cafe to see if there might be reason to have an early dinner. He just wasn't quite ready to eat. But the smells were working on him and the old woman wasn't about to give him coffee without a fuss. A booth by the window so he could watch the traffic go by. "Yeah, give me one of those specials," he said. "No fries."

"See, you must have seen the sign. You just can't remember, that's all."

"Well, maybe. A sign said Patty's Cafe. I remember that much. Are you Patty?"

She turned back into the kitchen and dished up two specials for the middle-aged couple. Balanced two heaping plates on her forearm and tucked a bottle of ketchup and HP sauce in her apron pocket and grabbed the coffee pot. "No I ain't Patty. She's my daughter. I'm Rose."

Scooted past him and placed the specials in front of the couple and filled their coffee cups and put on a smile that didn't suit her. Lipstick on her perfect white teeth.

John sat at the booth and looked out to his truck. Windrush on the dusty door. It made him feel not so far from home. A comfort in that glance and affiliation. Then he leaned against the window and looked down the highway in the direction he was traveling. Cool against his cheek. There on the gravel shoulder some kid sat on a hockey bag playing a guitar. He had a cardboard sign beside him propped up with two boulders. He couldn't read the sign.

A coffee cup plunked down in front of him. Coffee steamed. Two creamers tumbled like dice. "Fool kid's been out there all week it seems," Rose said looking out the window. Put her hand on her hip to balance the coffee pot in the other. "He doesn't use his thumb like the old days. Just sits with that sign flopping in the wind. No wonder nobody stops. Can't tell if he needs a ride or just singing to prairie dogs."

John nodded. He didn't feel much like talking. That road ahead of him. And after that he didn't know. But Rose didn't let his indifference sully her.

"No," she went on, "it's not my place. It's my daughter's. Her name's Patty. She can't work. She lives in the trailer out back." Jerks her head over her shoulder.

"Sick?"

"She's not well, that's a fact. Can't get out of bed on account of her weight. Nearly 400 pounds. I'm not fooling. Swear to God." Raises her hand like she's stopping traffic and looks skyward.

John raised his cup up to his lips and slurped off the hot slick from his coffee. Didn't care for weird stories or weird people. Thought they were the fodder for American prime-time television. Something that happens somewhere else. Then he wondered who was watching his salisbury steak. Turned towards the kitchen as if someone was there, to get Rose's attention.

"Shit," she screeched, "damnation!" She rushed back to the kitchen and scraped and slung and returned with a special still spattering on the plate. A slab of homemade bread to compensate for the overcooking. A square of butter. Fries, pickle slice and coleslaw. "Some bread to sop up the gravy," she said. "I'd forget my head if I didn't talk so much."

Made a face at the french fries. "Why is she so heavy?" John asked. Curious with such a calamity so near. Just behind the cafe. An obese woman living in a trailer. Ate his bread first.

Rose stood there and nodded. Not saying anything. She looked out to John Trickett's truck. Looked him over, considering if it was safe to talk to him. Something she wanted to say.

"She's had this place for ten years," she finally said. "Tom and Patty. A nice little business for them. One night two years ago they were having sex and Tom blacked out. A blood vessel burst in his brain. Died on top of her. Just like that. I had to take over while she grieved. She took to eating to deal with her loss. Some drink to numb themselves. Patty ate. Sad thing. No man will want her looking like that. I told her so."

John felt uncomfortable listening to such private matters. People he didn't know or care about. Just the same she was an amusing old gal. Talked a mile a minute. Seemed to a have a need for conversation when she wasn't in the kitchen. Wondered why she was working so hard at her age. Poured ketchup over his salisbury steak. Dipped his french fries. Ate them anyway. "Do you live with her?"

The orange cat walked in through the open door and dropped the mole on the linoleum. Rose stepped over and without so much as a pause kicked it out into the parking lot. A toe kick like a place-kicker.

"I think the mole was still alive," John said. Creases across his forehead. Dead for sure.

"I was aiming for the cat," Rose said.

She sat down across from him and pulled out a package of cigarettes and tapped one out and lit it with a dollar lighter. Red lipstick on the filter like some sixtie's starlet. "Hell no, I live down in Peebles. Had a farm down there that suffered through a few bad years. Overextended on equipment. Everything dried up and blew into Manitoba. My man shot himself for our misfortune. Jimmy. Shotgun in his mouth. Set it off with his big toe. An awful thing. And when the bank took back what they figured was theirs, I was left with a suitcase and my mother's china. I rent now. Drive up everyday to run this place and to look after Patty."

"Drive?"

"That old Buick out back. Glides like nothing these days. They made cars back then."

"It must be hard."

"Just living my life." Then her face went blank. Vacant. She turned to the window as if her hard life was just revealed to her. Stunned by the news. She inhaled her cigarette until the coal was plainly aglow. She disappeared somewhere. Peebles or that trailer that contained her daughter. Growing inside. Larval. The endless specials and grasshoppers clicking from the barren fields. She placed her cigarette in an ashtray. Her hands trembled and she clasped them tightly until her knuckles whitened.

John could feel the table moving, quaking. It seemed she was about to break apart. Struggling to hold herself together. Her personality fending off her circumstances. Frenzied distraction.

"I'm sorry," John Trickett said.

Rose sat there and finished her cigarette, then slid out of the booth and turned to him. A little sad. That edge softened. "Patty has no life. That's hard."

John looked up at her. His sad smile. Came in for a cup of coffee. Sit at a booth by the window and consider what was ahead of him. Even though he couldn't imagine what was around the next bend in the highway.

"There's a motel back a ways if your tired of driving," she said. "Cheap rates." Sensed she wasn't going to pry much more from her customer.

"Thanks, that sounds good." Suddenly overcome with fatigue. The thought of going home.

"If that fool kid's still out there, give him a ride, will you. I'm tired of feeling sorry for him."

John Trickett nodded. It was more out of courtesy. He hadn't decided if he was going to stay. He had to think of expenses. Just then a convoy of motor-homes pulled into the cafe parking lot. Must have seen the special. A crowd pushed through the door, joking, laughing. Men in beige and women in pastel slacks and floral blouses, retirees giddy with their freedom.

"Son of a bitch," Rose said under her breath, "would you look at that. I knew they'd come."

"Who are they?" John asked.

"Customers, by God. They've been staying away lately. We're damn near broke." She turned towards the door as they kept on fil-

chapter
SEVEN

John finished his dinner and washed it down with coffee then pulled out his wallet and thumbed a ten dollar bill and left it on the table. He turned to the kitchen and watched for a moment. Rose frantic and alone. Couldn't wait for change.

He went out the door and turned by habit towards the back of the cafe and noticed Rose's Buick. Mint condition. He was curious and walked up to it to have a closer look. It had an expired license plate decal. The cat followed him, arching against his leg as he stood there. It seemed that the car hadn't been moved in a while. It was covered in dust and the windshield hadn't been cleaned. He moved around to the back of it and there it was, the trailer, like a carton of cigarettes up on blocks. He could hear the wind sifting under it, moaning as if the heat was too much and it sought sanctuary there. It seemed to him a sad song and he listened, held his breath to hear it more clearly. A singing voice. Not the wind at all, he feared, but Roses's daughter wailing the dreary notes of her hard life. Perhaps a cry for help.

He stepped slowly towards the trailer and stood at the foot of the stairs outside the door. Looked around and listened for signs of life. A radio or televison. But there was nothing. He reached up from the bottom step and knocked on the trailer door. Lightly. No response. Then he rapped harder and called out. "Are you alright in there?"

ing in. Then she turned back to John and stooped down to him. Whispering to a confidant. "Look at the bellies on those old buggers. I can't afford to lose this group." Stood there with that red crooked smile. Lipstick cracking.

Winced as if it pained him to do so. Turned to the prairie dying. Wind chimes somewhere, the rattle of brittle grass and the grind of trucks eager to leave Prosper.

He climbed the stairs and pressed his ear to the door. It burned him and he pulled away. The hottest time of the day. Shaded it with his hand until it cooled and listened again. An empty tomb. Then an odd smell. Something foul and rotting. Many times in his life John Trickett had found stock felled by a rattler's bite or a busted leg from a badger hole, dead and bloated and roiling with maggots and a smell that would assault a man, grab him by the throat and choke him until his eyes bulged and teared. That smell of death. He wondered if she might be dead. Cooked in that hot box. Found himself in the middle of a crazy family. An old woman keeping a dead daughter. He tried the door but it was locked.

He banged on the door one last time and shouted into the trailer and pressed his ear against the door once again. That soft singing voice. Not words but sounds floating, plaintive, rising and falling. "Patty!" he called out.

No answer but that cheerless song. John stepped back to consider what to do. He thought that he should just tell old Rose, take a coffee for the truck and leave Prosper to its own affairs. But he couldn't just leave without knowing whether Patty needed help. He sensed something wasn't quite right about the situation. How could a frail old woman like Rose care for an overweight daughter? Then he thought he might peer through the windows and hurried to the back of the trailer. But they were barred and covered with dark curtains and shut tight except for one sliver of space in one of them. It was above his eye level so he jumped like a Zulu, but still he couldn't make out anything except the expanse of prairie all glaring and russet in the window. He was becoming anxious to know how she was. Now and then her mournful song rose up and it chilled him. Licked the back of his neck. Then he kicked at one of the timber blocks under the trailer and pulled it out and found a plastic milk crate. He placed the crate below the window and took the block and set it on the crate and propped it against the trailer. He climbed up on the block and leaned into the window and cupped his eyes.

All was dark and he waited for his eyes to adjust. After a time he could make out the door and something that had spilled thick against it. A puddle on the floor that seemed to have set like concrete. Or clothing perhaps, the pooling of a gown. A pale mass. He followed it with his eyes, fighting the edge of the curtain, bobbing his head to see what it was there on the floor. Then something symmetrical in the unrevealed form, bread dough rolled in two thin slabs. Triangular. Purple striations in old parchment. At the tips knobs and dark circles. Then his heart knotted in his chest. The naked body of Patty. Unmoving. Prostrate. Her skin spread out onto the floor as if she was poured from a vat. Breasts deflated. He stood back and fell off the block, but landed on his feet and turned towards the prairie with his hand on the brim of his cap and his mouth agape. Staggered like a drunk. Bowls of dust around his feet. Bent over in disbelief with his hands on his knees and bile churning in his belly. Thought he would throw-up. Then he gathered himself. A cowboy's swift recovery. No thoughts roused him to do anything but climb back up on the block. If she was dead, he wanted to make sure. A gruesome discovery.

Again he balanced himself on the wooden block and struggled to see more of her, knowing it was a body. A human form. Her arm wedged along her side. Skin from her torso folding over her forearm. A hand partially exposed. A finger. And the orange cat padding over her chest then sitting there to lick its paws and yawn. John Trickett had never seen such a macabre sight. But he kept on looking as if still not convinced of such a tragedy there before him. He wondered how the cat got in and strained until his eyes burned. And there near the door was a hole in the floor. Big enough for a cat. A lid from a tin can lay on the floor beside it. It seemed she had tried to cut through the floor to her freedom. But it was hopeless.

John lost all sense of time and place. His life. Only a hellish world in a dim room.

The prairie rushing away behind him to the ends of the earth. And then something moving alongside the heap of flesh, a hand rising. Moving heavy and slow towards the cat. The cat leaned into her hand and closed its eyes contentedly, unconcerned, unaware, only feeling that singular affection in all its purity. Patty was alive, barely it seemed. John banged on the window and called out to her and her hand left the cat and hung suspended, turning ever so slightly towards him. Acknowledging.

Then he jumped from the timber block and ran back to the cafe, a numbness taking hold of him, a primal directive to help, the essential part of him. The door to the cafe was still open and he rushed through the threshold and Rose was standing at the till behind the counter and those seniors leaning over their specials all slathered with ketchup tilting their heads to him dancing there animated and breathless.

Rose looked up. "We're closing," she said. Her eyes bouncing between John and her customers.

"Your daughter," John said fighting his breath. "She needs help. Give me the key to the trailer."

"She don't like strangers calling."

"Damn, woman, open it yourself. Just open it!"

"What were you doing back there?"

"She's lying on the floor. Cooking in that heat. What the hell is going on here? We've got to call an ambulance. Can you do that?"

"I think I lost the key."

"You lost it. When?"

"I don't know for sure."

"When did you see your daughter last?"

"Just this morning. You're sure asking a lot of questions."

"Your daughters dying in there. You couldn't have seen her this morning."

"I'm not sure."

"Where's your phone?"

John called for an ambulance. They'd be an hour. A bad wreck on the Trans-Canada. Started a grass fire. He could see that Rose was no help and there wasn't anyone else around except the seniors who just gawked like cattle. He strode through the cafe to the back room under Rose's protests. She didn't seem to grasp the gravity of the situation as she followed on his heels. He noticed a cot in a corner. Curious. Then a steel box filled with old tools. He rummaged and banged and removed a crowbar then turned to Rose watching like a child.

"Get two towels and a face cloth, Rose, and soak them good. Can you do that?"

She nodded and John ran back to the trailer and began to work on the door. Prying and pulling wildly. Then exasperated, he took the crowbar and pounded at the door knob. Clubbed it clean off and reached into the hole and pulled out the bolt and pushed the door. It would only open a few inches against Patty's body. She wouldn't last much longer in the heat and he removed his shirt and ball cap and leaned into the door with his shoulder and managed to open it enough to squeeze into the trailer. Out came the cat between his legs then a rush of fetid air, a furnace blast, rancid and stagnant. He stood over Patty, something heaved from the gullet of perdition. He turned back to the door as Rose slipped through with the wet towels. She seemed oblivious. Stupefied. Confused.

John took one towel and placed it over Patty's upper body. It only covered her collapsed breasts. He looked her over, what he could do. Vomit drying on her neck. Strands of hair clinging to the damp skin. He could hear her shallow breaths. The towel scarcely moved. Her mouth was open and her tongue was swollen. Lips cracked and bleeding. Her eyes were closed. Deep pits. She was lost in a shroud of skin, lashed with stretch marks like the bloodless veins of some parasitical host. The other towel he placed over her legs. Then he took the face cloth and wrung water into her mouth. Her tongue moved to accept it. Alive in that stretched hide.

"Just a little longer," John whispered. 'We'll get you out of here."

There was nothing to do but wait. It seemed she should have been dead. He looked around the inside of the trailer. How long had she been lying there, alone, starving, wasting? Dying. She lay in her own urine and feces. Baking in that vile way. Caked to her legs. One hand was covered in dried blood, swollen, like cooked sausages. The hand that gouged desperately at the floor. Empty boxes lay about her. Macaroni, dried soup, cans dented but unopened. A couch nearby was her bed. Another bed at the back. She must have tried for the door and fell unable to get up. Ate everything she could reach. Under the sink a copper pipe dripped. A small puddle on the floor kept her alive. Pulled her clothes off in the suffocating heat.

And then he noticed a prescription bottle on the floor. The cap on the counter. Anti-depressants. Then he lifted her head to reveal the soured contents of her stomach, curious blue dots disintegrating, the remnants of the bottle ejected by her body. He turned to Rose who leaned against the door with her eyes closed and her hands to her mouth. She slid down the door to the floor.

"What went on here, Rose?"

Tears streamed down her face, over her thin ravaged hands. She bawled as if for the first time in her life. Something went terribly wrong. "I couldn't do it anymore," she cried. "Doctors couldn't help her. There was no hope. Just this. She's better off…"

"She wants to live, Rose."

An old woman, tired and broken, reached into her apron and took something in her hand and held it out to John. The key.

"Take this," she said. Her eyes petitioned, a muted plea.

He took it as if some rare artifact was entrusted to him, the key to truth, the gateway to the Great Mystery. Some power bestowed to him. He placed it in his pocket then took up the face cloth and folded it and placed it on Patty's forehead. Waited for help.

The ambulance came and the paramedics tended to Patty. Oxygen and fluids. The Mounties arrived and John gave his account. He held onto the key in his pocket, rolling it over with his fingers. The deliberation of an honest rancher. Then he removed it and held it clenched in his fist. He wondered what had changed by his stopping in Prosper. What was the point of it all? Those old-timers watching him pass.

It took four paramedics to remove Patty from the trailer. A jiggling mound beneath a white sheet erased all hope. Rose followed behind, stooped and overwrought. Her dead child. A lady from social services held her arm.

The Mounties locked up the cafe. The seniors snapping pictures for the album. The sun was setting and John stood alone bronzed against the horizon darkening along the prairie margins. The air cooled. He wanted to leave in the worst way. Toronto seemed unobtainable. He got in his truck and rolled out across the parking lot and out onto the highway. That kid sitting on a hockey bag with a guitar in his hand. A piece of cardboard with Nashville scrawled in black felt pen. He had no obligation to give the kid a ride. He hadn't promised Rose that he would. As if that mattered. But there he was looking up from his outfit with his mouth hanging open expectant and eager as if she had arranged his parting. As if the ordered Universe assembled the characters in a play. Fashioned out of the prairie. John Trickett had no choice in the matter. Providence whispered to him. He stopped and reached across the seat and opened the door.

"I can take you to Winnipeg."

"I appreciate it."

The kid got in and John drove on following the moon quartering above the highway. An apple slice in the blue-black firmament. It made him think of heaven, not that he believed in it, but somewhere where Patty might be. At peace. "You want to be country singer or something?" he said. He didn't know what else to say.

"Yeah. I figured I'd try it."

"A man's got to start somewhere."

"You a rancher?"

"That's right."

"Must be a good life."

John looked off to consider his answer in the flashing-by prairie. The shadows of fence posts falling away and a kestrel picking the legs off a grasshopper. The world coppering. Ending. Trusted that it would be there in the morning.

"Yeah, it is," he said.

"What happened back there?"

"A woman took sick in the trailer out back. Her name was Patty. She died."

"Damn. I heard her singing at night. I played my guitar. I think she was following along."

"It might have been the wind."

"The wind is never that sad."

John Trickett turned to the kid and half-smiled. He didn't quite know why he did so. Perhaps it was the depth of what the kid said. It surprised him. Then he removed the key from his pocket and tossed it out into the prairie where the night crept in like velvet.

chapter
EIGHT

John Trickett pulled over at a rest stop near the Manitoba border for the night. A fitful night of engine brakes and high beams. In the morning the sun spilled over the hood of his truck like golden syrup. Blazed into the cab. Time to get up. The kid stretched and shivered.

John turned to him. Sizing him up. T-shirt and jeans and his sandy hair tousled and truck blown. "How long were you sitting out there on the highway anyway?"

"A few days, I suppose."

"That's a long time." He started the truck. The cab was heating up from the sun. Reached into the glove-box and pulled out a handful of peppermints and offered two to the kid. "Breakfast," he said. He turned back onto the highway. Flipped the sun-visor down.

"Yeah."

"You want to be a country singer. Have I got that right?"

"Yeah, pretty much. It's a long way though. It doesn't seem like I'm ever going to get there." He turned and laughed sardonically. His personal joke.

"My name is John Trickett." John offered the kid his hand. The kid wiped his palm on his dirty jeans and took it. Something yielding in his grip. It wasn't the hand of a farm kid, all thick and rough and firm. And farm kids acted different around adults. No slouch about them and all manners. The kid had a split lip and bruises about his slow eyes.

"Buck Kendall," the kid said.

"I have a friend with that name," John Trickett offered. He thought of Harley just then. Casual conversation without thinking. "His name is Harley Buck."

"Not related. If I was, my name might be Buck Buck. Sounds like a chicken, don't it?"

John turned to the kid grinning at him. A moment, droll and free, but sullied by something unknown to him, something about the kid all beat up about the face. Nothing to laugh at. His drowsy manner.

"Buck is just a nickname," the kid said with his voice trailing. "Same as my father. My real name is Brock."

"What happened to you? A fight or something?"

The kid didn't answer and John Trickett regretted the question. He only wished company on his journey. He didn't need to know anything about him, his troubles. Just company so he wouldn't be thinking so much. He had asked Rose about Patty and she told him some tragic tale that disturbed him greatly. Something he saw for himself. He just wanted coffee to go, but instead he saw life's hellish end.

The kid took up his guitar and strummed it softly. The window was open on his side and he looked out at the country passing by, duck ponds and the greening patchwork of Manitoba, playing so faint John Trickett couldn't detect a tune. Then the kid turned and spoke above his playing.

"Why do you think she was so fat?" He let his hands rest.

John Trickett turned back to the kid. It seemed that such questions were doors to other worlds. Something laying beyond, waiting to be revealed. He didn't care to know those other worlds. He was having enough difficulty just heading east, moving away from all that he knew. He left Prosper behind him and saw no point in discussing the life of someone he didn't know.

"Don't know," he said.

"She was in a lot of pain, I know that," the kid said thoughtfully. "Something awful she was trying to forget. That's my opinion."

"Could be," John Trickett said not leaving the kid much room.

"You're not an engaging man, are you, John?"

"Excuse me."

"Just like my old man, Buck Sr., won't talk about anything. He just skirts around things and hopes it will all go away." The tone of his voice became agitated and his hands leapt from his guitar, animated. "And if it won't go away, he just…"

The kid seemed sullen all at once. His head down. John watched him, curious about the look of him, his bruises. A kid out on his own. He wasn't much older than Del or Mitch.

"Sorry," the kid said. "I didn't mean anything."

John Trickett let the conversation fizzle. Implications sucked out the window like cigarette smoke. The kid pretty much figured him out. Not an engaging man. It had taken Harley Buck a few summers to fully understand that he didn't feel comfortable talking about private matters and a few more for him to admit that Nora had her grievances. Mostly Harley.

He felt bad for the kid's troubles. Sitting there slumped with his eyes closed, dozing with his hair blowing and dust settling on the dashboard from all that Saskatchewan top soil drifting into Manitoba, yellow along the horizon like distant fires. Following him east like the barn swallows. He ran his finger through the dust and bumped the guitar and the kid looked up.

"You play that thing?" John Trickett said. Benign talk. Safe talk.

"How far you going?" the kid asked.

"I'm on my way to Toronto."

"Business?"

John Trickett ducked. "I would like to hear you play."

The kid looked at him. Distrusting. "Yeah?"

"Really."

"What's in Toronto?"

"My brother. He needs my help. Look, I'm not a talker. I would just like to hear you play that thing. Alright?"

"Is he in trouble?"

"No, it's not like that."

"What then?"

"He has schizophrenia," John Trickett blurted out. He was growing vexed by the questions. It seemed he couldn't escape the kid's probing. "He's living in some ravine in Toronto. I have to find him and bring him home."

The kid just looked at John Trickett as if hurt by his impatience. Then he turned away to the safety of the window. "Sounds like a good thing you're doing," he said.

"I'm sorry. Just play." Shook his head. He couldn't talk about what might be ahead of him. The unacquainted horizon looming ever nearer. He couldn't talk about it and yet there beside him, a kid with a dream trying to encourage him. Fool kid didn't know the difference between virtue and guilt.

"My old man doesn't give a shit about my playing," the kid said. "Never did. He wants me to be a mechanic. Just like him. Kendall & Son Automotive. Finger nails all greased. Little black crescents. Dirty looking hands and reeking of oil. Not my kind of life. He figured if he beat the shit out of me, I'd change my mind. Dumb grease-monkey bastard. All it did was get my ass out of there. I'll show him. One day he'll regret laying a hand on me like that. What kind of man does that to his own son, Mr. Trickett?"

And there it was, some other world, that *don't want to hear it, ejaculate*. Something pouring out of his mouth, a spume of troubles filling up the cab. "Don't know," he said.

"Your old man ever hit you?"

"No."

"Did you ever feel like hitting him?"

"No."

"Ever hate him?"

"No." Exasperated at the kid's insistence. Had a flash of regret for picking him up. Cursed Rose and Prosper and long drives.

"I don't hate my old man. Hate is not the right word. I feel sorry for him. That life that's killing him. Grandpa Kendall used to hit him. My uncle Verne told me. Grandpa Kendall was a drunk. He would come home and pick on my father because he was the oldest. The right size for hitting. His brothers watched."

Then the kid went silent all at once and brought up his guitar and the neck knocked the rearview mirror askew and he began to finger the strings and sing. A slow seamless drawl like Alan Jackson. An edge of Merle Haggard honesty.

> *I don't need to say goodbye*
> *and weep my last farewell*
> *I don't need to stay and try*
> *to mend my life of hell*
> *I don't need to smell your rage*
> *when you raise your hand to me*
>
> *I don't need anything*
> *I only need to be*
>
> *I don't need your sad regret*
> *and promises that won't come true*
> *I don't need...*

Before the kid could complete another verse something along the roadside caught his attention. A coyote dragging its hindquarters was trying to pass under a barb-wire fence. All bloodied about the flanks. Tongue lolling as if half crazed of thirst. And John Trickett saw the coyote and glimpsed it as that truck bearing Windrush sped urgent and eastward.

"Pull over, John," the kid cried out, "there's a busted up coyote trying get out of that ditch. We got to help it!"

"There's nothing we can do," John Trickett said. "Nature will look after it. Critters are getting hit all the time trying the cross the highway. Fool things."

"Doesn't mean we should let it suffer," the kid persisted. "We got to help it. Come on, pull over."

John Trickett didn't appreciate the kid's tone but pulled over onto the shoulder as the kid was agitated as it was and now seemed more upset than ever. He thought it best just to go along with him. Likely the coyote wouldn't be there anymore. Dragged itself off into the brush. Or perhaps already dead in the ditch. He put the truck in reverse and backed up along the edge of the highway. The kid leaned out the window scanning the ditch for the coyote. And there it was caught about the neck under the bottom strand of the fence. Clawing with its forelegs as the truck stopped. Its teeth bared and menacing and black lips rippling along gums pink with bloody froth.

They got out of the truck and stood at the top of the ditch and looked down at the coyote that glared back from the corners of its yellow eyes. Pinned there before them, its kind snared in every manner and devise. Shot and poisoned and maligned. Road kill and no one sorry for the loss. Except the kid.

He pointed down along the ditch. Two dead coyotes with the black flecks of flies studded about bloody smears. "They're just young ones," the kid said. "This years."

"They must have tried to cross together," John Trickett said.

"We got to put it out of its misery," the kid said.

"He'll likely die soon. Just leave him."

Then the kid turned on his heels and went into the truck and rummaged around in his hockey bag and returned with a folding knife. He breezed passed John Trickett and down into the ditch and up the other side and stood over the coyote. He unfolded the knife and knelt down and reached under the chin of the injured dog and

it never moved or growled but seemed resigned to its fate. Brock
Kendall pulled the coyote's head back and passed the knife along its
throat several times until a crimson stream ran out into the prairie,
pooling black in the dust. He held the coyote's head until it bled
out and let it down gently and stepped away. He strapped the knife
through the grass like a barber until it was clean of blood and then
he folded it.

John Trickett stood dumbfounded at the ease the kid dispatched
the coyote. One minute the coyote snapped and hissed there in the
ditch. His gut trailing like sausages from a hole below its ribs. Then
all was done. Dead. The end of its suffering. Then he noticed the
kid looking out across the prairie. Some distance off, another coyote
stood in a rutted farmer's track watching them. Standing broadside.
It turned away and trotted a few steps then turned back. It was the
mother. Couldn't leave her pups. It turned away once again only to
stop and look back. It repeated the behaviour until the track disappeared over a rise and it vanished. Just the impression of it looking
back at two men standing over her dead pups.

"She led her pups all over this grand landscape," the kid said,
"criss-crossed with roads, rail and all manner of hazards. Bolted
across the highway and misjudged the speed in the glare of headlights. They had trusted her and followed."

John Trickett stood listening to the kid. Looked down at the
dead coyotes and out over the prairie to where the mother watched
them. A melancholy breeze rose up from the ditch. It aroused him
to wonder what had happened. Some meaning lying there to rot.
He thought of them, their lives, how beautiful they were around the
ranch in the winter. Their rich fur and thick ruff. Their unswerving
tracks in the snow along the frozen margins of Maple Creek and
the serpentine paths through the frosted willows. The one he shot
with the .22 he got for Christmas when he was thirteen. And how
he handed the rifle to Luke when the mate appeared from a hollow.
Luke was a crack shot. Told him to aim for the head, just behind

the ear, but the coyote suddenly reared back when it spotted them and he shot off a piece of its jaw. A spray of blood and teeth in the snow. They could never find it. A hideous crimson face wandering the plains until it starved to death.

chapter
NINE

He drove into Winnipeg and bought the kid a bus ticket to Nashville. He left him standing by the curb with his hockey bag and guitar. The kid out to make a name for himself. Rolled the window down in the truck and stuck his head out.

"One day I'll turn on the radio and they'll be playing Brock Kendall," John Trickett said. "That song you played for me."

"It'll happen, I know it," the kid grinned.

"You've got the right attitude, son."

"I hope you find your brother," the kid said.

"Yeah, Toronto is a big city." John Trickett's arms wrapped around the steering wheel and that inflection of doubt rose up automatically from that place he feared, the dark landscape of his undertaking, the utter futility of a cowboy stepping out of a truck with Saskatchewan plates aiming to save the Bug Man from his life of suffering. A newspaper clipping of Luke, lost for twenty five years. Perhaps long gone.

"You'll find him."

And the kid boarded the bus and John waved as he maneuvered his truck out onto the street. Shot down Portage and Main and crossed the Red River and fueled up at the outskirts, then hit the highway with the afternoon black and thundering and the kid on his

mind like a bur. Every reason to be mean spirited, another generation taught to hit what they feared. But he seemed to choose something else for himself, a disposition for compassion. Man, woman or
beast. His feelings for fat Patty languishing under the tomb of her
own flesh and his father who struck his willful mouth with knuckles
meant for his own father. And the coyote maimed and mangled that
he couldn't stand to see suffer, killed it slick then rose to face the
prairie and offered a eulogy to the mother for her massacred pups at
his feet.

He hit a stretch of bugs near Falcon Lake and then it started to
downpour and the windshield wipers smeared guts across the window so he couldn't see and had to pull over at a rest stop. Sat there
to wait out the storm. Turned the wipers off. A riot of drum rolls on
the roof and hood and rivers coursing diagonally across the windshield through the green slurry. He thought of Prosper and what had
ensued from a cup of coffee. A pebble in a pond and the rippling of
lives, touching, merging, immutable. A cast of characters come and
gone. John Trickett tried to reconcile such happenings but couldn't.
He just had an uncomfortable feeling about the kid. He wondered
why he didn't share his courage, his ambition. He had it once. Now
something lacking. And the rain pelted and outside the world was
obliterated and he felt very alone. He switched on the wipers and
glimpsed Ontario beyond the shredded curtains, dirty and flagging
and the sun splitting through and the forest thickening there at the
prairie margins. The world gaping. An invitation to enter.

He took a peppermint from the glove-box. Nora always bought
him a bag of peppermints when shopping in Maple Creek. Sucked it
like a soother against his canker. Nora would be making dinner for
the boys. Roast beef cut thick to feed their heavy work. There would
be talk of the day and then a silence filled with questions and the tic
of the clock that measured such awkwardness. Harley would be going on and on to Gerty about matters that galled him and she would
be simply nodding because she wouldn't hear a word of his prattle.

His mother and father sitting in their twin recliners watching television, some mindless show that would put them to sleep. Spent bodies slowly dying.

Sitting there in the truck he began to truly regret his notion to bring Luke home. Ambition born from some restless incursion of guilt. Now he just wanted to get back to normal, turn back to what he knew, to Windrush and cattle and mowing hay, tossing irrigation pipe with Del and Mitch, driving up to the Cypress Hills to watch the sun settle full-blooded over the western prairie, blathering with Harley about the weather and all manner of bovine culture and seeing to the dignity of his mother and father. And Nora, she would be standing in the kitchen drying her hands on a tea towel as he stepped through the door. She would look at him, smile because she would be truly pleased to see him back, but her eyes would falter and he would always know.

He slept in his truck in a parking lot in Kenora that looked out over The Lake of the Woods then got his breakfast at a Tim Horton's drive-thru. He looked in the rearview mirror as he pulled up to order. Looked a mess. Unshaven and hair like straw. Sprouted under his hat like a scarecrow. Sleep crusted in puffy eyes and his back ached. And a mood that usually shut him up for a spell.

The girl at the pick-up window greeted him cheerfully. "You're from Saskatchewan," she said. "My grandfather lives in Swift Current. He has a farm. Wheat as far as you can see. I'll be there in two weeks. Not much for me to do there, though. But my grandmother is sick and I want to see her. Windrush, that's a pretty name." Words like arrows in flight. Her eyebrows arching, waiting for a response, some acknowledgment for her enthusiasm.

John Trickett forced a smile. It was a mystery to him why some people just wanted to tell you everything. Felt uncomfortable around talkers other than Harley. Thought they were searching for salvation by spilling their troubles. He had enough of the woes and worries of strangers. No end of afflictions. He nodded, handed her a bill and took his change and coffee and timbits and nodded again. Rolled up the window and winced at his rude behaviour. A mute from Maple Creek. Likely her grandfather would hear about it.

As he drove through Kenora he thought he could have spoken to the young girl. There would have been no harm in that. The chances that she would have saddled him with some tragic chronicle was unlikely. A girl so young and cheerful couldn't have many troubles. It was her job to be friendly to customers and he didn't give her the time of day. Overreacted. He thought himself good natured. Tipped his hat to everyone in Maple Creek. Thought about turning around to get another cup of coffee. Ask about her grandmother. So he did.

The girl was surprised to see him. Still cheerful, undaunted by his manners.

"You're back so soon," she said.

"I was thinking that I better get another coffee," John said casually. Icing sugar on his chin whiskers. "Might not be another Tim Hortons for a while." Coffee and redemption.

She poured his coffee and handed it to him. He reached in his jeans for some change. "So how's your grandmother out there in Swift Current?" he asked.

"Oh, Grandma is not doing well," the girl said. Her smile fell away. Placed her elbows on the counter and folded her arms and leaned out the window.

"Sorry to hear that." Could feel the short distance between them thicken. Some other world. Dropped the gear shift into drive.

"Just old," the girl said plainly.

John Trickett sat there a moment. Ruminating. Relieved. "Well," he said, "getting old happens."

"I'm lucky," the girl said. I have a while yet."

He nodded as there were no more words to be spoken. Nothing left to offer. Just his simple observation. As he left he imagined everyone had a story. Some sadder than others. Tragic stories like his.

And as he drove deep into that new landscape of twisted pines

and rivers, those lakes and slabs of striated rock and sky clearing blue
and remote, he noticed how Windrush seemed to fade ever so slightly from his thoughts, the wake of his parting receding, diminishing,
occupying less of him, freeing him to look ahead. To Toronto. He
glanced up to the sun-visor and that picture of Luke. Standing on
a hay wagon with his shirt off. A big grin, muscles flexing. Tanned
and perfect and screaming life. That long hair that exasperated their
father. He took the picture with an insta-matic. Luke was looking
right at him with eyes clear as a spring, vitality born from the sweet
earth. Whole and unbroken. Always looking to him, to his older
brother. Their life ahead that seemed limitless, boundless as starlight
pinned to the infinite dome of the world. But a vision predetermined
to fracture and split. To lay ruined and wasted for all those years. The
hardest thing.

Past Ignace in the early afternoon. A truck pulled over to the side
of the highway with the hood up and someone standing near the road
edge. Nothing around for miles save for scattered farms and pines and
aspen along the hems of creeks and clearings. He slowed as the man
standing by the truck made a motion with his arms. John Trickett
noticed the back tire was flat. Beater with Ontario plates. And he
could see the man. His baseball hat with the peak folded like a half-
pipe and long hair to his shoulders. Thin mustache and sharp cheeks.
Lanky. Looked hungry. He didn't want to stop. Drove around him as
if he were passing a flag man at a construction site. Just ignore him.
It would be easier. Then he heard Brock Kendall screaming at him to
pull over. In his head, the guy needs help. Pull over!

He pulled over and the man walked up to his window. He
wouldn't have hesitated anywhere near Maple Creek. It was a prairie code to offer assistance to neighbours. Open space that could be
deadly in the winter. Drifts and blizzards. But there was no prairie along the clawed rim of the Canadian Shield, nothing familiar.
Not a neighbour in sight. Didn't know the ways of easterners. Even
Prosper, a prairie town of common folk, caused him great consterna-

tion. Nothing common about old Rose and fat Patty dead and gone. And Brock Kendall still seemed to be lingering along the wandering macadam of the Trans-Canada Highway. Silently cursed the inconvenience.

"I got a flat", the man said pushing his cap back, his eyes leaping all over John Trickett. ACDC t-shirt frayed around the neck. Teeth like a beaver.

"No spare?"

"Yeah, but it's flat too. My luck, eh."

Nothing to do with luck, John thought. "How far to the next town?"

"Well, about twenty miles to English River. I'm on my way there. My mother's birthday. She hasn't been feeling well of late. I could use a lift to get that spare fixed."

Everybody's mother. But John Trickett knew he had to help the guy. Out on the highway without a spare tire. Something odd about the whole thing. His nervous eyes. Would have to drive him back with the fixed spare and help him put it on. Then he thought about his own spare tire.

"Let's see if my spare will bolt up with your old Ford there. If it does, then you can just follow me into English River. Take it off at a garage and get yours fixed."

"Yeah, sure."

The man stood back as John took down his spare and rolled it to the back of the slumped truck. The man never had a jack or tire iron so he used his own. Loosened the lug nuts and jacked up the truck and removed the nuts and the flat tire and muscled his spare up to the studs and the tire slid on. Sweat dripped down his nose and hung at the tip like a pearl. Mashed his knuckles. Blood and grease and the lanky man stood and watched and looked up at a pair of ravens circling above them. Oblivious. The ravens throaty croaks and John Trickett swearing.

"They say they can count," the man said still watching the ravens.

His neck craned and his mouth agape.

John stood up and wondered if he could. "Follow me," he said walking back to his truck. He looked over his shoulder just as a car sped by. The man turned away and held onto his hat. He seemed to shield himself from view. Not wanting to be recognized. John Trickett stopped and stared at him and the man stared back. A moment of reckoning. Eyes locked in ambiguity, some vague allegation.

"My favorite hat," the man said grinning, "didn't want to lose it."

John Trickett kept looking into his rearview mirror. The man wasn't keeping up with the speed limit. Had to slow down so as not to lose him. He didn't feel right. He wondered how a man could be so useless. Didn't pitch in to help. Just stood there as if he had no idea what needed to be done. Never changed a tire in his life. Never dirtied his hands. The raw tops of his knuckles burned and wept and he wrapped them with a Tim Horton's napkin. He felt a fool for his kindness. Should have ignored the imposition of Brock Kendall flitting around the inside of his skull, that quality he possessed that made a man react without a proper evaluation. Wished he had Harley as a co-pilot. He would have identified the man as a laggard and waved him on.

English River ahead. He came up to a gas station and pulled in and stopped alongside a diesel pump. Got out of the truck and motioned to the young attendant. "Fill her up," he said. He looked behind him and nothing was there. No old Ford with a shiftless driver. His worst fear. He ran out to the highway and looked back to where he had come, then down the other way out of town. In the distance some truck rounding a bend. His spare tire on its way to wherever. He turned to the attendant who was watching him.

"The son of a bitch stole my tire!" John Trickett squalled. His face all red and twisted in some rare disfigurement of anger. He knew he shouldn't have pulled over. He just knew it.

"Stole your tire?" the attendant said. A pimply kid with a chin beard.

"I pulled over to help him and he steals my goddamn tire!"

"Ouch."

"You didn't see him?" John said walking back to his truck. "He was behind me." He turned both ways up and down the highway, across the street, turned completely around and took off his hat as if that gesture might lead to some explanation, absolve him of his poor judgement.

"No, didn't see anyone behind you."

"The guy had a flat spare," John said, his voice piqued and racing, "so I put my spare on his truck and he was to follow me into the garage to get it fixed. He was behind me all the way. I must have dozed or something. Didn't notice that he kept on going. Said it was his mother's birthday and she wasn't well. Some lame story. I went for it. Can you believe that guy? Dumber than a chicken. Do you have a police department?"

"The OPP in Upsala."

Leaned against the box of his truck and hung his head. "He's long gone." Looked up to the attendant. Blood nearly drained from his face. "Do you have any tires that'll fit my truck?"

"Well, we just sell gas here. Back around the corner there's a tire shop."

"What?"

"That guy have an old Ford that's seen better days?"

"Yeah."

"Sonny's got a truck like that and he comes to town to visit his mother. He's not that smart either. Some kind of sickness when he was just a baby. Everyone knows him."

The crunch of gravel and John Trickett turned his head while he leaned and lamented about his misfortune. That old Ford and the man getting out. He waved and turned to the back of his truck and retrieved John Trickett's spare. Rolled it over to the gas pumps.

"Hey, Sonny," the attendant said.

Flashed his buck teeth. "Here's your spare, mister. Thanks a lot, eh." The attendant helped him hoist the tire into the box of John Trickett's truck.

John's mouth gawped soft and useless and no words could be formulated. He didn't know how to respond, what should be offered. Stepped back from his truck and looked around. Confused and addled as Sonny stood there before him. As if he had suddenly lost his bearings and his purpose. Lost in the smothering forests of Ontario. Longed for prairie dogs and heat waves and ponds surrounded with nothing but blue sky and bellying clouds piling white along the horizon. An unencumbered life.

Then Sonny lumbered back to his truck, all arms and legs. He reached in through the window and pulled out two bottles and ran back with them tucked under his arm like footballs and handed them to John Trickett. "Thanks a lot, eh," he said once again. He looked down at his feet then over to the attendant and shrugged. That mute from Maple Creek.

"No problem," John said at last. His voice trailed as if a hairball caught in his throat. He couldn't look him in the eye and gave one of the bottles a spin to read it. Sonny Merlot written in pencil on a blank lopsided label. A handy diversion. He gave the attendant his credit card and paid for the fuel. Got back into his truck and placed the bottles on the seat next to him and took a peppermint from the glove-box. Took him for a thief and an idiot. Never thanked him for the wine.

chapter
TEN

John Trickett stopped in Thunder Bay and had soup and a sandwich at a Tim Hortons. It evoked familiarity, a suggestion of sentiment. The girl at the drive-thru in Kenora had grandparents in Swift Current. Tenuous ties to home that assuaged him. He sat in a booth and rarely looked up, mantling his dinner like a hawk on a vole. He decided he didn't know a thing about people and saw no need to be sociable. There were complications that he couldn't see by plain observation. Harley Buck had that gift, but he had no such discerning quality. He worried how that limitation might come to bear in Toronto. Another day and he would drive into a city of 5 million people to find one man among them.

He could feel others watching him. A foreigner in their midst. He thought of Sonny Merlot. As if that was his last name. He laughed out loud. "Sonny Merlot," he snorted. Shook his head. It had been a while since he laughed. Then he grew self-conscious. Didn't like to be stared at like some fool hick. But he hadn't shaved or bathed since he left Maple Creek and he smelled. So likely he was a sight. He left with four cups of coffee in a tray and a maple-cream doughnut for his sweet tooth. Caffeine to help him drive late into the evening.

He passed the Terry Fox monument with his likeness and that hitched stride that John Trickett and the rest of the country would always remember and out there a lake that went on forever like the prairie. A sign read Sleeping Giant, something resting in the bay, the sun coppering upon its flat crown. And a ship glided above the vast water in the distance, an illusion, like those seductive pools of water shimmering on baked Saskatchewan asphalt. And the sea of Lake Superior lapped at the wilderness and on and he drove into the twilight, skirting that great lake there on the Courage Highway but felt no braver for it. It seemed that Ontario would never end. Town after town and cold coffee and moose crossings. Bridges and rivers and headlights flashing and his eyelids threatening to slam shut for good and finally he turned off the highway and stopped for the night at Marathon. A motel and a late call to Windrush. The phone rang five times before Nora answered it.

"Just me," John said. Sat down on the side of the bed and fell backwards. Dug his toe into his heel and pried off his boots. Flung them.

A pause before her voice began. Conversing via satellite. "You haven't called. I was wondering if you would."

"Long days."

"Yeah."

"How are the boys making out?"

"Just fine. They have Harley watching over them. He came up the drive in his truck but stopped halfway. Lost his nerve. Turned around and five minutes later called over on the telephone. Wanted to know if Del and Mitch needed a hand. Must have seen me at the window."

"That's funny. I can see him doing that." Images of home. Common things. It felt like he'd been gone a month.

"Mom and Dad?"

"Same. Walter's been exposing himself to the nurses."

"Scary thought."

"Do you think I'm a bitch, John?"

"What?" Just a word, but always with so much venom. A word

that assaulted, blamed. Harsh and overused. He closed his eyes. She was never that.

"I just don't think I can do it. It's all I've been thinking about."

"Don't think about it."

"It's no small thing."

"I know it's not."

"You sound tired."

"Yeah." He brought his hand up to shield his eyes from the lamp on the night table. Somebody talking in the hallway. Laughter. Footsteps and voices fading. A dream image slipping into his consciousness. At the cusp of sleep.

"You didn't answer me."

"Yeah, I'm tired. I better go. Toronto tomorrow. Give my love to the boys and Mom and Dad."

"I will." Receding, falling away from him.

"And Harley too."

"He'll shit himself."

"I know."

"Are you alright?"

"Yeah."

"Okay."

"Bye."

He took his coffee down to the lake in the early hours, showered and shaven, clean jeans and his jean jacket shoulder slung. He was ready to go on the final leg. He called Alex Grove, the reporter, and she gave him directions to a hotel near the Don River. The Bug Man's lair. He marked it on a map of Toronto. Arrows along the highways and city streets. She would meet him at Starbucks on Yonge Street the following morning. That new-age coffee shop. He walked out onto a dock and stood at the end of it and admired the fine boats. The unbroken breeze from Superior brought in rollers and he watched as the sun gleamed across the bottle-green crests, one after the other, rising, swelling and then curling against the shore dispersing the shattered bits like beads of glass. The sound of the world in motion. A kingfisher perched on a snag above the water. Swallows and gulls disappeared into the trough of waves. The smell of boat gas and lake water. An organic blend.

He sipped his coffee. It always helped him consider things. Thoughts would emerge. How to mend a split irrigation pipe or the merits of Angus, Belgian Blue, Charolais, Limousin or Simmental herds. But now his mind was all but empty of Windrush and all those chores that kept him outdoors for twelve hours a day, seven days a week, empty of that old routine. Except the sound of Nora's voice.

He missed her. Her making things happen, organizing, managing. His security. Loved her in the long grass on the banks of Maple Creek. She struggled with the thought of Luke. Her fears. What would happen if he did find him and brought him home? He didn't know. The future that he could not predict or prepare himself for. He just needed to keep moving forward. To go where he feared. That one thing.

chapter
ELEVEN

The thickening of farms and towns and the air growing heavy, sticky, sweat trickling down his back and the strands of his hair lying dark and wet against his temples. He rolled up the windows and turned on the air conditioning. Past Lake Simcoe looking for Highway 404. Those eyes that studied the emptiness of the prairie, the unrestricted sweep of it with deliberate and thoughtful attention. Suburbia patched with Victorian homes and grand oaks and maples and new streets stained with strip malls. There a Tim Hortons. And then Highway 404 and he could feel in his bones a quickening, a sense that something loomed beneath the smudged sky, redemption or folly. He was there or he was not.

John Trickett had no detailed plan to find Luke. He would leave that to what Alex Grove could tell him and providence. Though he was not a religious man, he hoped that some power might assist him. It seemed the closer he got to Toronto the more anxious he became. He found himself praying, not to some deity, but for help of any kind. An appeal to something he could not define. It emerged as his fears intensified, some response that surprised him. He wasn't sorry for it. It kept him heading south, there without Nora to reassure him. That strength of hers. And the wisdom of Harley Buck all but useless. Harley knew the secrets of hay and hoppers and prairie dog towns but would be rankled to fits of scratching when at last in the late evening the CN Tower glared like a golden idol above the urban hordes of Toronto.

The Don Valley Parkway, following the arrows on the map. A river valley splitting neighbourhoods, gouged down through the wooded slopes, serpentine and slow, a green gash in the heart of the city. The ravines under a forested canopy. If someone lived in the shadows there, he could not say. Missed the Bloor Street exit. Didn't even see the sign. He followed the flow of cars like liquid down along the Don River until he could see glimpses of water. Toronto Harbour. As lost as he could be. The map folded and useless. He thought it best to stay on the parkway as the city loomed and he didn't relish the notion of driving the labyrinth of congested streets. The parkway turned west along the waterfront and he knew he was heading back toward Saskatchewan. The Gardiner Expressway was so long that he thought he might find Maple Creek at the end of it. He turned north and an hour passed and he managed to negotiate an interchange that seemed improbable. And to his amazement he found himself back on the 401 and soon the Don Valley Parkway off-ramp. This time he was careful to look for the Bloor Street exit and slowed along the white edge line like an Albertan. He found it sure enough and pulled over onto the shoulder and stopped, relieved and exhausted. He closed his eyes and rested his head on the steering wheel. Circled the globe.

Then the Bloor Street exit and a traffic light and a panhandler approaching cars. Others on the periphery, dodgy. Mostly the drivers ignored the thin panhandler. His stained shirt and sleeves ripped off and both arms tattooed down to the wrist. Hair cut with a weedeater. Patchy beard. A hand came out of the car in front of John Trickett and handed the panhandler a bill. He smiled and nodded some gesture of appreciation.

Then he moved to the big Ford idling and rattling. John rolled down his window. Thought it best to accommodate him. Managed to retrieve a few quarters from his pocket and reached out to the panhandler. He took the quarters and stared at them in his dirty hand. The dark pits of his eyes. An expression of disbelief. Gratitude, John imagined. Then the panhandler raised his eyes to meet John Trickett. Feral like a cat, piercing, distrusting. His mouth open showing his yellow bottom teeth. Thick with plaque.

"You cheap fuck, Zeke," he said mordantly, then tossed the coins over his shoulder.

The light turned green and John never moved and the car behind him honked and startled him and he punched the gas pedal and shot ahead, shocked and speechless. Unnerved. It disturbed him to such a degree that he had to pull into a gas station to gather himself. Felt he didn't deserve such harsh words for his offering. A dollar in quarters. He wondered what the panhandler expected. Get a job. It was an outrage to think that filthy beggars could dictate levels of his charity. Soured him. He opened the glove-box and took a peppermint and the newspaper article. Something about the panhandler. He scanned over the article and that picture of Luke. Someone in the foreground and the caption: '*He's a freak,' Steven says.* It was a winter photograph and he was wearing a coat in the final stages of disintegration, a size too small. He could see what appeared to be a tatoo fringed around a tattered cuff. He would know. The panhandler would know if Luke was still living in the ravines.

Toronto was a city on a grand scale, filling his view in every direction with colour and textures and rhythmic sounds of movement like the rush of a river. The din of the multitudes. Towering buildings a few blocks away and traffic thick and stalled in the twilight. Red taillights like his father's cigarette butts. He pulled back onto Bloor Street and finally arrived at the Gardenia Inn. Left his truck in a parkade. Laboured out into the mugginess that slammed against his chest and packed his throat with hot wadding. Thought he could chew the humidity.

He checked in and flopped on the bed in his room and channel surfed. A couple making love. Some tanned guy with a mullet hairdo moaning as he thrust up against a woman from behind. Rehearsed rapture. Breasts like inverted bowling pins swinging in and out of camera range. Cheap music made for such occasions. It made him feel uncomfortable to watch. Felt unclean somehow. Nora wouldn't mind it though, he mused. She said things like that would help him. He thought of calling her. Another channel. A farmer from Weyburn who talked about his problems with the drought. The cracked and forsaken pasture of southern Saskatchewan. A life from his past. Back to the tanned guy with the unhinged pelvis and the stamina of an Alberta oil rig. Back to Weyburn. Toronto at last.

In the morning he stood before a brick building on a corner. Starbucks. It looked old. And when he went inside the faces seemed young. Alex Grove waved him over to her table. Stood up and offered her hand.

"You must be John Trickett," she said.

"You could tell?" His wheat pool cap and jean jacket that he wore in all weathers. He sat down and glanced around the room, to the assortment of people drinking from mugs and paper cups. The gathering of the world. A table of thin black men with small heads. They wore robes. Felt panicky. Pushed his cap back and exposed a white forehead but wasn't self-conscious of his farmer tan. Wondered what planet he landed on.

"Are you alright, Mr Trickett?"

He turned to her. A stranger talking to him. Short blond hair that was more yellow and pale milky skin. A heavy girl wearing black lipstick. Earings climbed her ears like ladders. Dressed in black. Seemed too young to know anything. He had no prairie to carry his eyes away and was forced to notice. He noticed his long breaths trying to calm himself. "I'm kind of out of my element," he said.

"I'll get you a coffee," Alex Grove said. "Cream and sugar?"

"Yeah, sure. Thanks." Sensed there wouldn't be bacon and eggs.

She got up and stood in line. Looked at her watch and then to John Trickett and smiled, a city anomaly.

John had the article with him and removed it from his back pocket, stuffed in there like his Watson's. He unfolded it and ironed it on the table with the edge of his thick hands. And when Alex Grove sat down with their coffees, he set the page in front of her and pointed to the likeness of Luke.

"I'm looking for this man," he said. "I think he might be my brother." Thought he heard an other language behind him. Half-turned. Distracted. He took a sip of his coffee and made a face that he hoped Alex Grove didn't notice. Something strong. Nothing like Tim Hortons. "Do you know if he's still in the ravines?"

"Oh, the Bug Man. I only saw him that once. I could never catch up to him. No one could. A city works crew found his camp and tore it apart. But they say he rebuilt it."

"Rebuilt it?"

"His glass fortress. He liked to collect things. Bugs in jars. Out all night. Hid in his camp most of the day. Kind of spooky, don't you think? I wanted to interview him, but they say he was long past the interview stage. I mean no disrespect if he is your brother, Mr. Trickett, but he seemed pretty sick. Most of the ravine dwellers were afraid of him. But that was then. I haven't been back since."

"Has anybody?"

"Street workers and street nurses."

"Is there any word of the Bug Man, some news of his whereabouts?"

"I write a travel column now, Mr. Trickett. I'm just not involved with the fringes anymore. It was like I wrote this article and expected that it would lead to some miracle of healing for those people. Yes, I was obsessed with idealism. My ego had grand plans. God, street people would be eternally grateful to Alexandra Grove, emissary to the impoverished. I felt like Dian Fossey venturing into the jungle. But, I think her gorillas were more civilized."

"You sound a bit disappointed." Thought she meant Jane Goodall.

"I just told the story. I didn't help anyone."

"Well, I'm here on account of it."

"Excuse me for saying so, Mr. Trickett, but you don't seem equipped to deal with the ravine dwellers. This isn't Saskatchewan. You're not in Kansas anymore." She laughed at her cleverness, but quickly regretted it.

"I suppose." His shoulders sagged involuntarily. The truth of it. But he had come too far to sulk over impediments. In fact it seemed a victory to John Trickett, to be sitting there at all. "I just need to see if he's still here," he continued. "Find out what I can. If he's down there, I'll find him. He's still my brother." Persevered and showed her the picture of Luke on the hay wagon.

"Good looking guy." Recovering.

"Yeah, he had everything going for him. A future. An entomologist. That's what he wanted to be. Study bugs."

Passed the picture back. "You be careful down there, Mr. Trickett."

"I think I saw one of them back at the traffic light. Near the river. A panhandler. Looked like this guy here." Pointed to the newspaper.

"That's Steven. That's his spot. Swears like Ozzie."

"Who?"

"Just stay away from him. He's a bad one."

"They're in the picture together. He must know something about Luke."

"Listen to me, Mr. Trickett, he told me something I'll never forget. Chilled me to the bone. His words cut with such cold certainty. He said that if he caught the Bug Man, he'd break one of his jars and hack out his throat. His eyes popped out at me like hard-boiled eggs. I believed him."

"But why?" His face folded. Couldn't comprehend such brutal threats.

"Something. I don't know. Something he did to Steven. And he won't forget it. I know that much."

"He could have been just shooting off his mouth."

"Yeah, some of it's just talk. Threats and intimidation. Mr. Trickett, there are those that will carry out what they say. They don't know consequences. Doesn't occur to them. Steven is like that."

"Didn't the police know what was going on down there?" Hated the panhandler. Noticed his hands squeezing and his molars grinding, a rumbling deep down inside him that made him feel sick to his stomach.

"They knew that street people lived there."

"Why didn't…"

"Look, Mr. Trickett, I wish I could help you more, but I have to go."

"I thought you might take me there." Held his hands out. Appealing.

"I can't. Just go down into the woods at the traffic light. You know where that is. I hope you find what you're looking for."

"My brother," he said firmly. Was there something else?

"I hope he's not your brother." Eyebrows of black liner arching. She stood up and pushed her chair back and looked away from him and walked towards the door. As if she did not want to feel his offense. Her brazen opinion for his own good.

She left the coffee shop and John watched her pass along the windows and then he turned causally to the unfamiliar faces of every ethnic curve and shade, all races collecting there around him. He wondered if he was still in Canada. All those languages. But no one seemed to mind. He sat there with his coffee watching people come and go, drumming his fingers on the table, mindful of what Alex Grove said about Steven, 'stay away from him,' mindful of his threat, some crazed intention to kill the Bug Man. His mind fastened to Steven like velcro, there simmering at Yonge and College at the end of the earth where worlds diverged. He wondered how he would approach him. And then a young man with long hair braided in frizzled ropes came through the door. He wore a t-shirt and on it read: *Bring Back The Don, Save the Lower Don River Watershed.* And then his fingers stopped.

chapter
TWELVE

John Trickett stood off to the side of the road near the traffic light where the panhandler pitched for his piddling alms. A wooded embankment sloped downward into the broad valley of the Don River. The impenetrable lattice of leaves formed a canopy that hid the earth from Bloor Street. No sign of Steven, not a trace of fringe dwellers. Where were the homeless? He imagined them all under that verdant screen clinging to trunks of hardwoods enduring their marginal lives. Billeted to a world out of view, without civility. He could not imagine beyond that. He did not know the origins of the indigent, how they came to slide into the shadows of Toronto there below him. Such questions invoked no compassionate eye with which to see. He did not share the ideal that inspired Alex Grove to care for just a little while. Simplicity of motive. Bring Luke home. It did not require a study in cultural anthropology, humanities, economics, social phenomenon and urban demography, nor did it compel him to undertake analytic comparisons between Tim Hortons and Starbucks. As if prairie simplicity had identified two types of people in the world according to John Trickett. Canadian culture reduced to something recognizable.

And then in a break in traffic, bird song trickled down from the high crowns like a tumbling stream. The sharp hum of cicada.

And someone vaulting up out of the woods waving and yammering. Steven sprinting up to him. Slipping and accusing.

"Claim-jumper," he shouted, "get the fuck away from my spot!"

John Trickett held up his hands. He knew he had to be discerning. "I'm not after your spot," he said.

"It looks like you're about to set up shop. No one works this spot. Especially hicks."

A hollow faced kid perhaps in his late twenties. He had a high-toned nasal quality to his voice. Dirty pockmarked skin pulled away from his eyes making him appear older. Pouchy and hungry. A life on the street. Dirt under his fingernails like a mechanic. Thought of Brock Kendall's father.

John Trickett afforded him a wide margin. "I'm not after your spot," he repeated.

"Then what the fuck are you doing here?"

John looked out over the valley. Squinting against the sun. "I've just come to see the river," he said. "I'm here to help bring back the Don. That's all."

"I remember you," Steven said. "You're that cheap Zeke."

"That was all the change I had on me," John confessed truthfully. Turned back.

Steven ran his eyes up and down John Trickett. As if measuring his worth. "A tree hugging Zeke," he said. Walked up close to him. Glaring. Lips curling contemptuously. "Why don't you just leave the fucking river alone. Leave us alone. Bust those polluting pricks instead. Go after the politicians instead of planting a thousand fucking trees. I see them down there along the trails. Homely chicks with pony tails. Urban wilderness. Spiritual rejuvenation. Solitude from society. Friends of the Don. Singing and dancing. Digging in the mud. They'll be forcing us out of here. Then what? Back in the fucking alleys with the addicts and their rigs. Dumpster diving. Maybe to Vancouver to shiver in the fucking rain. Who gives a shit, eh Zeke?"

Steven didn't seem stupid or muddled. It was true, he had a fond-ness for profanity. Nora used such words to stress some point she felt keen about, but Steven used them in a hateful way. John sensed an intelligence behind his lashing out at the world. He feared him, his anger. Thought of Alex Grove's warning.

"I care what happens to the people down there," he said. Working his way towards Luke.

"You're from out of town, Zeke," Steven said patronizing. "Saskatchewan plates. You don't know dick." Pulled a plastic bag of cigarette butts out his pocket. Looked like a bag of shrimp. Chose one and placed it between his teeth and lit it with a zippo lighter. Strands of his moustache, melted, curled.

"I know the Bug Man will likely rebuild his camp if the city takes it down again," John said lowering his eyes in that moment of nerve. His heart flailing in his chest for such daring. Then he raised his head cautiously and was met with Steven's feral eyes boring into him. The grim cast of his mouth expelling some acrid seed. Crossed some line there at the verge of the Don Valley. The portal to madness.

"What do you know about that freak?"

"Oh, I don't know anything. I just hear things. Some say that he lives in a glass house."

"Fucking jars."

"I'd like to see it. Him too."

"What for?"

"Curious, I guess."

"Well, he won't be there."

"Why, do you know where he is?"

"Why do you give a shit about the Bug Man?"

"Help him."

"You want to help him? Some piece of shit Zeke from Split Lip. No one helps anybody down here, though I suppose street workers help some. But the hard core fuckers like that Billy Bum and the bug freak, can't help them. Better off dead. Just shoot them in the head."

Raised his hand like a pistol and pulled the trigger with his index finger. Made a noise like an explosion.

"So, have you seen him?"

Steven's eyes pressed to slits. Wary. Stepped back.

John Trickett felt he was about to lose him. Had to think of something. Some Harley Buck wisdom. "There's been a sharp decline in Mourning Cloak pupa this past spring," John said. "I hear that he knows his bugs. Would like to talk to him. Butterflies are important to the Don." Remembered the dream he shared with Luke those many years ago. The health of ecosystems. Pollinators, essential to the vitality of the planet. A zoological mystery. And Windrush would be the model for ranchers and farmers on the southern prairie. A mission for the young and brave.

"I think you're full of shit."

"The truth is," John Trickett said lying again, "he has to leave the ravine. Part of our clean up. I didn't think that you would tell me his whereabouts right off. Protect him from outsiders."

Steven sneered. He looked around at the traffic backing up. Clients. The sidelong race of his eyes holding John Trickett like a spider's web. He seemed to consider the merits of ridding the ravine of the Bug Man, speculating that John Trickett might be useful.

"I went down there, Zeke," Steven said, "just once, to see his glass house for myself. It glows at a certain time of the day. When the sun is just right. Eerie as hell. I surprised him in his lair. That's what it seemed to me, some fortress of some kind. I was right on him. I can be real quiet when I want to. He shit himself. He had something in his hand and it wasn't his dick. Some green thing. He flung it at me and it hit me in the face but it didn't glance off. I could feel it moving. Something alive. I reached up with my hand and it was this huge fucking bug. Like a stick. I pulled at it and it clung to my beard. I panicked, dancing and clawing at it, yelling at him to get it off, but he just stood there. The dumb bastard had no expression. I finally managed to pull it off and threw it on the ground. It was a praying mantis and it must have been six inches long. Creepy fat tilting head. Eyes like peas. I told him right there that if I caught him outside his jar house, I'd kill his sorry ass."

"Doesn't seem reason enough to kill a man."

"See for yourself if you wait long enough. He'll be along."

"You have seen him, then?"

"I said that I couldn't catch the fuck. I didn't say that I hadn't seen him."

"I think I'll wait for him."

"Suit yourself, Zeke. Stick around for all I care. Maybe you'll see the freak run over. Just don't be crowding me."

Steven left John Trickett by the rim of the Don River Valley and went to work along the line of cars idling and jerking there on Bloor Street. He pulled a folded sign from his back pocket that read *Spare Change*. Some ignored him and others reached out as if they knew him. Regulars that tolerated and supported his panhandling. Not much effort required, John observed, other than slouching about like some refugee rejected by the world. That and more gall than pride. He left the lip of the Don and sat down on a corner of the concrete bridge abutment and watched Steven moving among the cars and noticed that he began to limp, one leg then the other, as if he had been afflicted with some ailment that had the ability to move through his limbs at random. Conjured up to invoke charity from the most prudent. He didn't seem bothered by his vocation. Earning a living. Now and then casting a derisive glance towards John to affirm that even that spot had been territorially pissed on. And then Steven looked to the wooded ravine with a wild vigilance. Expectant.

A breeze rushed up from the Don River and John Trickett turned to it and closed his eyes. A relief from the heat and traffic noise. The rush of rapid transit. Sirens in the distance that seemed all around him, stitched the city together with emergencies. People needing help. An epidemic. He felt sleepy, lazy, unmotivated to move. Thoughts rising and passing. Didn't like being called a Zeke. Had the urge to slap Steven's foul mouth. Then he opened his eyes and at his feet a dandelion rose up from a crack in the concrete, a weed by all accounts, that sulphur yellow head unworthy of flower status. He stared, fixated on the colour against the neutral tones of concrete, the inert grey mass of industry. The will to live, the push and pull to survive, to be in the world. And how a honeybee came to find it there, a sun for its faceted gaze, pollen baskets on segmented legs. Just the way Luke used to see things. Shrink down into the world of bugs and live among them. Appreciate them. Marvel.

He rested with his elbows on his knees like a boy with nothing better to do. And then Steven called out and he raised his head as someone darted out of the woods and raced to the front of the line of vehicles and disappeared. So swift the person was that John doubted that he had seen anything at all. But Steven confirmed that he did as he stepped away from the cars and trucks and marched up the road shoulder cussing.

"You fucking freak," he shouted, "get lost!" He picked up a stone and held it cocked in his fist then stealthily crept like a cat stalking freedom and turned to look between the cars as he went.

John left the concrete abutment and ran up towards the traffic light to see what the commotion was all about. The Bug Man he surmised, and Steven was bearing down on him with his all his enmity. His rage and spit. Searching him out along that perilous progression of cars. Then John stopped, stalled and uneasy, as Steven flushed the Bug Man from his crouch, kneeling before cars like some Detroit devotee. Horns sounded and the Bug Man jumped back and Steven hurled the stone and struck him in the back and he spun around and grimaced and fell and struggled to gain his feet, pitching forward with his hands like some simian. He scurried for the woods, sliding down the slope and before he vanished into the woods he looked back over his shoulder to John. A fleeting instant where eyes lock, where lines of vision cut distance like lasers and the brain translates milliseconds into recognition, familiarity, truth or perhaps deception.

"I'll kill you, you retard!" Steven shrilled.

John Trickett said nothing. His heart pleaded for retribution. The cruel strike of the rock. Steven's words diminished. Lost.

"Now do you see what he's up to? He reaches through the grill and picks bugs from the radiator. Fresh and dried to his liking. Only he would think of it. I wish the stupid fucker would get run over. Rid the world of such shit."

Still did not answer. Could not yield and burn. His mind was occupied with that surreal figure swallowed by the Don River Valley. Was there a likeness to Luke, something familiar concealed in the Bug Man? Beneath the matted hair, behind the beard that covered his face like moss encroaching, creeping over the remnants of skin. Obliterated all comparisons to Luke that he held in his memory. And clothes filthy grey and ripped and patched with plastic bags and bits of cloth, taped together in some pattern mimicked from his mind. A spectacle of chaos and disorder, his illness manifested on the outside as if it had crawled out of his mouth and birthed a wretched hide of sickness. And those eyes that fell upon him. He removed the picture of Luke and studied the strong confident eyes. Looking at him. Could it be?

Then John Trickett managed to dislodge his tongue and called out after the Bug Man, a desperate petition to all that he hoped for. "Luke!" he shouted, his voice cracking, breathless, trailing. "Luke," he called out again, "Luke Trickett." It echoed flatly from some remote valley brim. But there was nothing. Nothing resolved. Nothing gained. And as he stood looking out over the mystery of his life he felt Steven come up behind him.

"Who are you, Zeke? Who the fuck is Luke Trickett? It just doesn't make sense for some farmer to be messing around down here. What do you want with him?"

"Nothing."

"Hey, Zeke, don't fuck with me."

John Trickett turned on his heals and grabbed Steven by the neck of his threadbare shirt nearly lifting him off his feet. His fingers thick as bananas from a life of ranch work. "My name is not Zeke, asshole," he said. "Do you hear me? And the Bug Man just might be my brother Luke. You lay a hand on him, you'll answer to me. You got it?"

They stood nose to nose with cars carrying on behind them unaware of the drama unfolding along the city margins. At the cusp of a parallel world. John Trickett teetered there, neophyte to the shadows of Toronto, clutching the keeper himself. The incubus that he never imagined, breathing his vile breath. The heat of it. There at the crossroads of a fool's journey. Perhaps, but still he knew he had to venture down into the keeper's gullet to find Luke. To go where he feared or not at all.

chapter
THIRTEEN

He stood by the window looking out over the city. There was nothing else to do in the room other than channel surf. But that was tiresome, up and down searching for something that might appeal. A scan of humanity. Tragedies at your fingertips and enough commentary by thin haired men to solve the inexplicable. Problems of the world exposed and visceral. And in all that opinion and politic no one was talking about the Don River people. Some race discovered in the ravines of Toronto. Just blocks from the CBC, the Bug Man slipped in and out of the shadows like a thief. Stooped before cars to snatch the paper-thin hulls of insects sucked through molded plastic grins. Soon he would leave to find the truth in the Bug Man's camp. Luke or some chimera.

John Trickett liked to take his coffee out at the barns. Lean against the blood red boards his father nailed and look out over the prairie and speculate about the day. Always he turned to the sky to see what weather might come. Harley did the very same thing, as did most ranchers. It was a time to appreciate the stillness. The silence. And the beauty of light and shadow creeping along the textures of Windrush. Nora would join him after a time, her coffee cradled in her hands and a sweater wrapped around her shoulders. She afforded John those moments by himself. Just a few minutes together in the morning then they would toss their dregs like cowboys and go off to work the sun down. A ritual that he thought about as he watched the sun catch the glass panes of office towers. Something he had done every day of his marriage but rarely considered notable. He longed for it now, the simplicity, the routine. The comfort of his home. Then he had to let the thought go. No time for melancholy.

There was complimentary coffee on the dresser. A drip machine with a pouch of coffee and sugar and whitener and a styro-foam cup. A plastic stir stick. He tried it and returned to the view of Toronto and the gold plated windows that suddenly dimmed and the sky dark and gathering. Thunderstorm in the forecast. He couldn't finish his coffee and poured it down the bathroom sink. Drinking coffee in such a manner lacked ritual. He put his boots on and left the hotel and strode down Yonge Street. Rushed along by the rumble in the distance and the need to resolve the mystery of the Bug Man, galvanized by what Steven told him, what he saw. Angered too, by Steven's callous affronts. His derisive tongue and queer ginger eyes.

He stopped at Starbucks. Couldn't find a suitable alternative. He left with two paper cups in a tray and a cup in his free hand, past Maple Leaf Gardens heading towards Cabbagetown. There were those who smiled as they passed. Others did not. He felt starkly rural and raised his urban coffee to appease them. Young girls with exposed midriffs. Made the best of men look. He sipped his coffee while he walked. Strong like a boiled down pot of Nora's kick-starter. He guessed that he might be preoccupied in the ravine for a spell and unable to attend to his habit. He didn't smoke or swear and only drank when Harley encouraged him. The need for coffee at regular intervals was about as depraved as John Trickett would ever be. Though he surprised himself when he grabbed Steven by the throat. His anger just rose up and took hold of his hand, a will to shut him up. But there was a stronger feeling that wanted to squash him like a bug, some judgement he had deep down that he didn't know was there. It spewed out of his mouth like a gush of oil from some secreted vault. Retchings of outrage. It was a startling revelation. He rarely raised his voice to anyone. To his father of late, out of exasperation. Fear of such frailty. To see what he was to come. And Nora, her stubbornness was enough to vex a man, but it was something that he admired in her. That attraction. And she was right most of the time when it came to disagreements. Except when it came to Luke.

Steven was working the cars of the morning rush as John Trickett stood staring like a jumper down the grassed slope to where he last saw the Bug Man, that meeting of eyes, a connection that could not be reconciled without proof. To leap into the arms of providence. Luke was somewhere down in that serpentine underworld of myth and lore where the mists of the Don River smoked like the slavering breath of some beast. And the jar house waited for the sun to bear down upon it, a warning to trespassers, or perhaps a beacon for a prairie pilgrim coming to liberate the cracked soul of a man. A brother.

"You're waiting for the sun to come out, aren't you, Zeke?" Steven said walking over to John Trickett. "To see that fucker's porch light. Right about this time. Too bad it's clouding over."

John looked skyward and Steven snatched a coffee from his tray. "Hey, what the hell do you think you're doing?" John said stepping away from him.

"You shouldn't have," Steven said.

"Well, I didn't."

"I thought you brought me a coffee, Zeke. Some of that hick hospitality." Sipped the coffee slow and deliberate. Some rare commodity.

"That line of yours is getting mighty thin, Steven. It is Steven, isn't it?"

"Yeah, but I don't think you've earned the right to call me that."

"And you think it's alright to insult me? Steal my coffee?"

"That's what came to mind. Just a name. And take your fucking coffee. Who drinks three cups at once? You're a strange fucker." Held the cup out and sneered.

"Keep it," John Trickett said. Puzzled over Steven's runaway mouth. Some sickness.

"It's been a while since I had something hot," Steven said. His mordant disposition seemed to slacken. The corner of his mouth lifted. Delight over a rare pleasure.

John watched him. Heedful of a chameleon's changing colours. Like Luke perhaps. He considered asking him to take him down into the Don to the Bug Man's camp. But he did not trust Steven, did not wish to be near him, his wildness like a creature condemned to scratch and slither a confined existence. Fanged to live another day. He turned away and began down the grade into the Don. He called out as he walked. "My name is John. John Trickett."

Steven ran up to the edge of the slope. "John Trickett, brother of Luke Trickett," he shouted. Turned back to the line of commuters and cupped his hands around his mouth. Mimicked a barker. "Step right up folks, tours now leaving for the Don River in search of the Bug Man. Just follow that Zeke in the jean jacket. Pride of Booger, Saskatchewan."

He wanted to distance himself from Steven. He was unpredictable. There was no telling what he would do to Luke if they came upon him. Spun a horrid scenario. Steven bashing Luke with a broken jar. Then he reached the bottom of the slope and entered the sunless woods, the canopy above him a dappled shawl dusky and alien and he was seized by the foreboding of an unacquainted world. In the stillness of the deciduous groves bird song fell silent against the waterfall rush of the Don Valley Parkway. The air was cool, oxygenated. He turned to look over his shoulder to make sure Steven wasn't crouching there like a panther. But there was no one on the path. Nothing moved. Leaves hung still as death from unmoving twigs and branches black and frozen. Still he had a queer feeling that he was being followed. Some shadow slipped behind the fissured trunk of a maple. So many places to hide, to conceal oneself. There was no such places on the prairie. It was if every move was witnessed by the Universe. There was nothing that could be kept from Maple Creek, from Harley Buck.

The path left the brooding woods and the overcast sky seemed bright and comforting. He could not see the metropolis of Toronto, the bustle and chaos. It was there, although it was hard to imagine, a million beating hearts beyond the forested bluffs. Soon other paths merged, separated. There along the river a couple walked holding hands. A man on a bike. Dogs on leashes. Where were the fringe dwellers? Then behind him, the drag of a foot. A breath. A blue jay scolding. He swung about and faced the screen of impenetrable woods. Never had his eyes been bound by the limits of geography, the sky squeezed into a circumscribed gap, a mere filet of prairie horizon. Place and time fused and he felt lost in that sameness where nothing could be seen beyond the pathways of the Don. And then he glimpsed a patch of blue through an opening in the trees. At the mouth of a ravine sliced into the base of a wooded bluff. Some encampment he guessed and he moved towards it along a narrow worn trail. Someone would surely know the way to the Bug Man's camp, someone other than the contemptible Steven.

A scrape in the woods and two young men huddled under a blue tarp looked up at John Trickett. Startled like refugees exposed and found. Garbage spilled out from the shelter. Wine bottles and candy-bar wrappers, a sundry of paper and squashed beer cans curiously scorched. Candles burnt down to tin lids. The odious smell of excrement. Hatched out of ruination.

"Hello, there," John Trickett said casually. One foot up on a stump and an elbow across his knee. Pretentious ranchers. "Sorry to bother you. I was wondering if you've heard of the Bug Man."

"Some," the kid closest said. The other swiftly hid his face behind him and clung like a suckling primate. A monkey-boy. A hooded pullover and a sleeping bag torn and stained around his shoulders.

"Do you know how I can get to his camp?"

He pointed upriver without taking his eyes off John Trickett.
Didn't seem to approve of the intrusion.

"How far?"

"A ways."

John sensed he wasn't going to get much more than that. He
had figured it was a ways when he left the Bloor Street Viaduct. He
stood there in the awkward silence breathing from his nose and noticed something in the monkey-boy's hand. A glint of dull light. He
looked hard into the shadows of the shelter and could see nothing
but his sleeping bag. And then something withdrawing. Or nothing
at all. Then the kid looked past him as someone broke through the
trees into the camp.

"Hey, Steven," the kid said flatly.

"Billy Bum, how's your new boy-toy?"

"Leave him alone."

"Zeke, what are you doing with these fags?" Steven's fox grin.

John Trickett screwed his lips at the question, uneasy, considering
what was there before him. Two kids camping in filth. Then he felt
his hand coming up. Thick fingers flexing.

"Shut up, Steven," Billy said.

Behind him the monkey-boy moved. Shrinking.

"Just looking for directions," John said. His head down at his
feet. Could no longer look at Billy and his companion. An unsettling revulsion.

"Well, you won't find that here in this crack shack. They only
know one thing and they don't need directions to find it. And they
don't know what the fuck you're talking about, Zeke."

John Trickett had to leave. He felt panicky. Nausea creeping up
into his throat. "What are you doing here?" he said, his words sput-
tering nervously. The impulse to shake the life out of Steven worried
him.

"I couldn't let you get lost down here by yourself. You might get
hurt."

"Well, that's thoughtful of you."

"Saskatchewan farmer disemboweled by ravine people in Toronto. Police suspect foul play." His voice deep and articulate like a news anchorman reading the evening headlines. Then the whites of his eyes like a lunatic.

"Funny."

"He's along the Belt Line trail," Billy said. "A couple miles. Up near the Brick Works."

"Thanks," John said. The slight turn of his head towards Billy. Then he turned away from the wretched encampment, avoiding eye contact with Steven. But all at once branches began to thrash and lightning struck down like a portent to some perilous venture. Clouds whisking in hurried dashes and rain began to fall in heavy sheets and the riotous pummeling of leaves and tarp was deafening.

John Trickett and Steven took refuge under the tarp with Billy and the monkey-boy as the skies disgorged. Mud jumped from puddles and leaves of oak and maple glistened and danced and dripped. Rivulets ran through the camp indiscriminately and smelled of septic. Water trickled down John's neck as he crouched there in the company of young men disparate and alone looking out at a world through the partitions of censure and gloom. Deviants all. A palpable hopelessness.

In the din of the storm Steven weeded out a sizeable cigarette butt from his stash and lit it and smoke palled and settled over John Trickett. Billy pulled out a cigarette of his own and lit it and passed it to the monkey-boy. He smoked it heavy and passed it over his shoulder to Steven and he smoked it until that sordid refuge was filled with a blue haze. The smoke smelled hard and pungent like the spring burning of straw and fence posts. John knew what it was. He thought back to those days when Luke would roll fat joints that made them giddy and hungry for peanut butter sandwiches at midnight. Luke was partial to marijuana while he favoured alcohol. How many times had he found Luke in the morning with a slice of bread stuck to his face? And then Steven passed the weed to him and he returned it to Billy. No words were spoken. A ceasefire in that sharing of space and hemp.

chapter
FOURTEEN

He took a hot shower and washed off the ravine stink. Soaked to his skin from the downpour. Smelled like compost. He sat on the bed wrapped in a towel

"Could you just get Harley, Gerty," he said. "It's me John. Yes, Gerty, John. That's right. Is Harley in from the barns? Alright, put him on." Held the telephone away from his ear and rolled his eyes. Some things vexed him. Infirmity.

"Damn, John, we were beginning to think they don't have telephones in Toronto."

"I phoned once, Harley."

"Yeah, I know you did. And I'll tell you plain, John, it troubled Nora. To see her fret like that. And I know it was nothing I did. None of my business. But still, you being away from your folks and Windrush. And that scheme of yours. I don't know, friend."

"Yeah."

"That's it?"

"How's my mom and dad?"

"Well, they could either charge Walter with indecent exposure or put him in a hospital. They chose the latter. And your mother's in a hospital in Swift Current. Sad state of affairs, John."

Stared down at the worn carpet. Guilt driven like a spike into his stream of thoughts. Created a gap that he rested in, a fleeting moment without thinking of anything. Thinking was risky.

"You should be home right now, John."

"Yeah, I know it."

"Hell of a time to be away."

"I know what I left behind, Harley. It may not make sense coming out here, but this is what I should be doing. Don't get me wrong, I have my doubts. About everything. Mom and Dad, well they've had their lives. Luke hasn't had a life. I can't think about it any other way."

"And Nora and the boys?"

"Del and Mitch; they never knew their Uncle Luke."

"Nora, John."

"I'll tell you, Harley, it's a hell of a thing to have to choose between your brother and your wife."

"Yeah. Well, have you found him?"

"Not quite."

"What do you mean, not quite?"

"He's around. There's those who have seen him."

"Luke?"

"The Bug Man."

"That likeness."

"Yeah, but I'm certain it's Luke."

"So how have you been holding up, John? You sound tired."

"It's a screwed up world out here, Harley. Never seen so many sorry lives." Remembered the people along the way. Rose scratching out a living in Prosper; her daughter Patty nearly 400 pounds. Swear to God. A sad death. And Brock Kendall running away from an abusive father and Sonny Merlot standing lazy and buck-toothed by his wreck of a pickup truck. Flat tire and no spare. The melting-pot in Starbucks and now ravine people.

"No disputing that fact."

"Just this morning down in the ravines, smack in the middle of

Toronto, I spent three hours with a couple of gay fellows and some lunatic named Steven. Swimming in filth. Stunk to high heaven. Here I thought they were two young guys camped out. Turns out they're homosexuals. Right in front of me embracing each other. Pissing rain and surrounded by their own shit. Never seen the likes of it, Harley. What's wrong with these people?"

"I suppose, John, if they knew a better way they'd be doing it."

"I don't know. No way to live."

"That neck of yours, John."

"I'm no redneck, Harley. Come on, you know that."

"All I'm saying, John, is that it's showing some. I never knew you to be one to judge a man. I'm a little surprised."

"You think so?"

"I do. It's not like you."

"You're not the one being tailed by some crazy man. Threatened to kill Luke."

"Steven in the newspaper?"

"Yeah, I think he wants to follow me to Luke."

"You're worried about it?"

"Worried as hell. Believe he'd do it."

"A man's got to keep his enemies close, John. That's all I can say. I'm not there with you."

"That's all Dr. Buck can come up with?"

"You forget that I was overseas in Normandy in 1944. Just a kid. A lot of boys died not knowing where the Germans were. Same on both sides. I've seen the worst of men and the best of men in the same minute. Keep him in sight, John."

"Thanks, Harley. I better go."

"Alright, do what you got to do, cowboy. And know that men have a tendency to punish women with their silence. Remember that."

"Yeah."

He lay in his bed while the storm continued outside. Knew what Harley said was true. All of it. Thought of Billy and the monkey-boy hunkered down beneath the leaky blue tarp. Cold and damp. The riot of trees. Steven had a camp nearby made of plywood stolen from a construction site. Orange tarp draped over the sides like a square pumpkin. There were other camps he noticed on his way out, hidden enclaves of cardboard and scrap wood and plastic sheeting. He did not see them at first. They seemed to materialize out of knowing that they were there. Manifested by observation. A woman appeared before him on the trail. Mouthing some gibberish. She was wet from the rain and the strands of her hair stuck like leeches to her pale skin. A biblical narrative stuck in the loop of her affliction. A cross clutched in her hands to dramatize her rant. Made him want to run. The Don River Valley was a dismal place in the rain and muck of ruined lives and he was happy to be snug in his hotel room. He pulled his mind out of the depths of it and visited the Cypress Hills. Popped into his mind out of nowhere.

How he used to gaze out over the prairie contemplating life and all its complexion. He chuckled to himself. His world that he walked over, knew every step. The smell of sage and the taste of dust on his tongue. That outer world. But there was another world he sensed, that place Harley eluded to. He said that it wasn't like him to be so judgmental. If it wasn't like him, then who was it like? John thought he knew himself. Just then he realized that he didn't know anything at all. Had no answers. Exiled out of the only world he knew, that simple life shaped out of the constricted space of Windrush. Routine, weather and worry. Worn like his jean jacket, a skin that began to split along the repetitive seams.

John Trickett could see that the rain stopped. He went down to the hotel restaurant for dinner. Ruminated over a steak sandwich what he would do. Finally he decided that he would go to Steven's camp and ask him for help. A venture that seemed ill-thought, but he believed what Harley told him. Keep him close. Besides, he had no idea how to find the Belt Line Trail or the Brick Works. Down there in the suffering groves. He asked the waiter to box the other half of his steak sandwich. Throw in a couple of dinner buns. He left the restaurant and bought a package of cigarettes at the hotel gift shop. A postcard of the Hockey Hall of Fame building and a stamp. Would mail it to Harley when he got the chance. Stopped by his truck and scribbled down some sentiment and tossed the postcard in the glove-box. Then he grabbed the two bottles of Sonny Merlot's wine and two empty Tim Horton's paper cups. An offering to temper Steven's volatility.

He retraced his steps to the ravine like some emissary from a world set apart. The dinner of the fugitives. This time he did not feel so lost, intrusive. A fish out of water gulping impotently. Down through the trees that dripped and hung like listless hands. That dusky sunless place. He hurried there then followed the path of the sane along the river, those urban strollers from the city. Kindred of civility. He veered to the bluff and found the orange box of Steven's camp. Away from impressionable eyes.

"Hey," John Trickett called out as he neared the camp. "Steven."

A hand reached out and took hold of a corner of the tarp and pulled it back. Steven stuck his head out. "Zeke, what the fuck do you want?"

"I thought you might be hungry."

"I bet you did."

"No, really. I couldn't eat it all. I didn't want to waste it. Steak sandwich. Some buns."

Steven looked up at John. He licked his lips. Couldn't help it. The smell coming from the styro-foam box. The bottles of wine and the paper cups. "It's that Bug Man shit, isn't it?"

"Yeah, I'm not going to lie to you."

"You don't give a shit if I go hungry, really, do you?"

"No, I don't."

"Don't bullshit me, patronize me or feel sorry for me. I fucking hate that. That victim shit."

"I won't."

"Then give me that."

"I brought some wine."

"You shouldn't have."

"I know it."

He ducked under the tarp into Steven's shelter. Pervading orange. Steven's scowl as he took the boxed sandwich and opened it and stuffed two buns into his maw then motioned with his hand to the bottles of wine and paper cups. John understood and peeled the foil from the crown of one bottle and took out his pocket knife and dug out as much cork as he could then speared the remainder into the bottle. Poured wine into a cup and Steven took it. Washed down the buns and spat out bits of cork.

John sat down on a milk crate and looked around the shelter. Avoiding Steven's eyes. A queer semblance of order. Newspapers stacked in the corner. A mattress covered with quilts. Wooden boxes served as tables. Cardboard floor. Thick candles like feed silos. A recycling bin filled with wine bottles and beer cans. And a bookcase made from planks and bricks and along the spines of books he read: Journal of Medicine, Human Anatomy, Medical Student's Handbook, African Mythology, Journey to Africa, Man's Search for Meaning. And on top of the book case a framed photograph of a black boy. Big eyes, dull, emotionless, lifted to the photographer.

Steven did not say a word until he was finished eating. Picked up the wine bottle. "Sonny Merlot" he said. Turned the bottle around. "Best served with panhandlers and fat-assed Zekes."

"How is it?" John said ignoring the comment, his eyes not leaving the picture. Something compelling there.

"Try it yourself, Zeke. You brought another cup."

John did bring two cups but didn't fully appreciate that he might drink with him. Never planned that part lest he reproach himself for such guile. It wasn't like him. But Harley sanctioned such behaviour. Said to keep your enemies close. And John had done just that.

"Here," Steven said.

John held out his cup and Steven poured. He took a drink and it warmed him down into his belly. A nostalgic feeling. Drinking in old Grandpa Trickett's shack on the lip of an aspen coulee near Windrush. A view of trembling leaves and Luke falling out the window into a saskatoon berry bush. He had left him there and laughed until his sides ached.

"Not bad," he said. He reached into his coat pocket. "Smoke?"

"Damn, Zeke." He tucked the cigarette behind his ear.

They sat in silence sipping. Steven watching John Trickett, suspicious. Sat on his mattress, leaning forward, alert. Then it began to grow dark in the shelter and Steven lit the candles. Shadows danced against the orange tarp, prelude to some tribal offering or perhaps the souls of the mad unhinged and free to reel against the night.

Alcohol worked its way into John Trickett's brain and managed to dislodge his tongue. He was looking at Steven's books. "What are you doing here anyway?"

"Who cares?"

"You seem smart enough. Why live here?"

"Do you know somewhere better, Zeke?"

"Anywhere but here."

"Ever been to Africa?"

"No, why?"

"Forget it."

"Alright," John said.

Steven was abrupt and guarded but not in his usual caustic way. It seemed to John Trickett that he was hiding from something. Hold out in the ravines.

"Who's that black kid?" John said. A slight nudge for his curiosity.

"Don't matter. He's probably dead anyway."

"Why do you say that?"

"Because he's from a fucked up country in a fucked up world."

"Africa?"

"Yeah," Steven said solemnly. He took a bite from the steak sandwich then put it back in the styro-foam box and placed it under his quilt for safe keeping. "You don't want to know about Africa," he said.

"You were there?"

"Yeah, I was there."

Wine poured to the brim.

"Something happen?" John asked. The question came innocently enough. Just passing time. Showing some interest with the hope that Steven would be agreeable to take him to Luke's camp. Never considered that he was a traveler.

Steven's shoulders slumped and he stared down at the floor and his eyes withdrew darkly. A mood that John Trickett could do without. Things were likely to get worse and he began to think he should leave before they did. Didn't care to be that close to one of his tirades. Might have to shake him senseless. That anger.

"I should go," John said to assuage such unease. He got up and stooped with his back against the ceiling.

Steven raised his head. Something longing in his ginger eyes. "No, don't," he said.

John hesitated for a moment, then lowered himself slowly back onto the milk crate and sat there watching him. He placed his elbows on his knees and laced his thick fingers. "You don't have to tell me about it," he said. Father to son. A sudden sentiment stirred by Steven's capricious nature and alcohol's deception.

There in the silence of that orange cube Steven drank from his paper cup. Wiped his mouth with the back of his hand and nodded.

chapter
FIFTEEN

Steven reached to the bookcase and took the picture and held it with his two hands. "This picture," he said, "just a beautiful child. Not yet a man. There's nothing else to see." Turned it to show John Trickett.

"Those innocent eyes," John said.

"What we can't see doesn't mean it's not there."

"What do you mean?"

"Fear." Steven lit his cigarette. Looked at the length of it between his fingers.

"What was he afraid of?"

"He was holding a machete. It was covered in blood. The shorts he was wearing were soaked with blood. And it wasn't his. Behind him on the side of the road bodies lay strewn. All hacked. He was afraid that he would die like those he helped kill."

John Trickett's mouth parted, confused and disturbed by such a claim. Just a picture of a black boy. It couldn't be true. Steven couldn't be trusted. A story to entertain him in a gruesome manner. But he could see that all was not show and fabrication. Steven's jaw still shivered by the telling of it. The absolute sobriety in his voice.

"What were you doing there?" John said. Beginning to worry now by things he didn't know. The grave furrows of his own fear. The flash back to a news-clip overshadowed by weather and hockey scores and the smell of roast beef.

"You might think I'm full of shit."

"I didn't think you cared what I thought."

"Maybe I do."

"Alright. Just don't mess with me. I just might get drunk and believe you."

"Open that other bottle, Zeke."

John Trickett poured the rest of the first bottle into Steven's cup, then opened the second bottle. "Does this mean you'll take me to Luke?" he asked. Looked down into his cup. Left Steven some room.

"You could have asked Billy Bum to take you," Steven said. He pinched off his cigarette and put it in his bag of butts. "Habit," he said.

"Yeah, I could have."

Steven nodded as if some meaning was left unsaid but understood. A bargain struck. His eyes flashed prophetic in the candle light. He placed the picture back on the bookcase. Something symbolic in the flame licking the picture glass.

"My father is an elder at St. Andrews," he said. "He comes by once a week and brings me his old newspapers. He doesn't say much other than, 'when you coming home, Steven?' A sad man since my mother died. The church keeps him busy. Presbyterians aren't ones to be idle. A whole world to save. Heal the suffering and all that."

Steven spoke a whole minute without swearing. Didn't spit his derisive offensives. The even timbre of speech. Contradicting.

"I wouldn't know," John said. It was true that he didn't. Walter Trickett could never afford to dismiss two strong backs on Sundays. Though he kept a Bible just in case a drought had dug in like a mule. Pulled out all stops at such times. John's mother went to church alone after Luke vanished. And she prayed a great deal. But John thought that was just the grieving that would never leave her. He wasn't down on religion. He just never had time for its formality. In fact, he felt those evenings alone in the Cypress Hills was a type of religion. He talked to the stars. And he recalled how Luke talked that same way to aspens in autumn. Quaking leaves, like golden coins against the deepest blue sky. Luke speculated that such beauty might be God.

"Believe me, it's true," Steven said. "I finished my first year in medicine at McMaster University in the spring of 1994. My father made sure that I had no time off to stray and pledged my service as a medical assistant in Rwanda. There was a tribal war brewing there, incited by rebels, and the World Help League sent out a plea for students. Why not? I didn't know anything. Been nowhere. A week after term papers I found myself in some village amidst the worst genocide since Hitler, the systematic murder of villagers. Machetes and masus. Kill or be killed was the edict. Boys like him.

"We were stationed in a field hospital. Treating survivors. Limbless men and women wandering like zombies. Buzzards followed the killing like clouds of hell. That colorful clothing and gaping pink slits in arms and legs. Heads split open like melons. It reminded me of that scene in Apocalypse Now when they butchered that water-buffalo. Do you remember that?"

John didn't move. Couldn't.

"Anyway, we stitched them up the best we could. We heard horrific stories of women who served as sexual slaves. Raped with rifle barrels and sticks, mutilated then murdered. Fear had so consumed the people that they turned in their own families and watched them die. We didn't know who was fighting who. And we didn't know why.

"The scale, the scope of such butchery began to affect me. I couldn't sleep. I became increasingly anxious. I felt panicky. Like I was losing my mind. But there were those among us who fared worse. There was a young girl from my father's congregation who went with me. A nursing student named Claire. She had a camera. Took that picture. One night the rebels came and took her and her camera. She managed to remove the film. They placed her in an abandoned house. Dead bodies were stacked in the living room. Flies. The smell. In the pile of corpses one hand moved from beneath. Someone was still alive. She stayed there and held that hand. A man or a woman, she didn't know. She held the hand and stroked it all through the night and in the morning that hand went limp and cold. The rebels destroyed her camera and after much deliberation released her. She possessed a depth of compassion that truly was a marvel. She said that it was a privilege to share the end of one's life. I think it saved her.

"I remained in Africa for four months then returned home to continue my studies at McMaster. But I couldn't do anything. I couldn't hold a thought. I fell into a deep depression. My father counseled me. Then a shrink. Medication. Another shrink. I began to work at St. Andrews helping out with the homeless. My father's idea. Serving food. I took food down into the Don River, here, that autumn. Some guy in a lean-to invited me to stay. He was so happy with his meal. His first in a long while. He had Aids and was dying. He was so composed, withdrawing from the world on his own terms. He said that he had seen the other side and that it was good. I visited him a few times and then one day he was gone. They found him in the river. I guess he just decided it was time. Returning to the womb. I sat in his shelter that day. The river wanted me too, but I fought against the pull of it and just listened to the silence. Listened to the woods. Nothing lasts in this world. Everything is impermanent. I suppose that's what I learned."

John Trickett sat still. Something scurrying across the tarp. The world exploding in his head. He felt a vague sense of hopelessness. What's the point of it all? What those old-timers seemed to say in Prosper. He took a long drink. Then another. The scurrying inside his skull.

"Well, Zeke, now you've heard my story, what about you?" He pointed to the pack of cigarettes in John Trickett's pocket.

John just stared at him, not quite sure who he was looking at. It was if Steven were two separate people. The contemptible panhandler and the humanitarian. Which one was he? The grounds for his loathing seemed to shift beneath him, his supposition called into question. John removed the cigarette pack and tapped out a cigarette for himself and gave the rest to Steven. His inebriated grin.

"Why don't you just go home, Steven? Sounds like your father wants you back." John Trickett lit his smoke with a twig set alight from a candle.

He lingered on the sound of his name. Validation."The truth is," he said, "I would if I could. But something happened to me in Africa. Something that just won't heal. I've heard of it happening. Not everyone."

"What?"

"Sometimes when a person is subjected to intense horror and terror over a period of time, the patterns of their brain can be irrevocably altered. It happens to soldiers even when they are prepared for such things. I wasn't. Had no idea. Just a Canadian kid with big dreams who landed in the middle of a holocaust."

"Wouldn't you be safe at your father's house?"

"I'm not good in public. I have these rages. Blow up over little things. A shrink told me he thinks it's some kind of defense mechanism trying to protect myself from the horrors I've seen. My brain interprets small things as something threatening. I swear. I yell. I go a little nuts."

"No shit. Why not here, though? You seem different."

"Nothing can threaten me here. The world's out there. I've found sanctuary in being alone. Believe me, Zeke, it takes all my energy to get up to Bloor Street where I show the world this crazed kid. To keep it at bay. Intimidation for a few coins."

"Why were you following me yesterday?"

"Don't know. You need help and perhaps a part of me still wants to help people."

"My brother Luke needs help."

"How does a brother of a farmer like you end up here? Tell me that."

"I'm a rancher," John said a little disgusted and drunk.

"Whatever."

"Luke has schizophrenia. He walked away from a half-way house twenty five years ago."

"The last time you saw him?"

"Not exactly."

"What, then?"

"My parents had him committed to an institution near Vancouver."

"Did you go see him?"

"No."

"And you wonder why he walked away from that half-way house."

"Yeah."

"Fuck, Zeke, I had the impression that you were close to your brother."

"We were best friends."

"But you bailed on him."

"Yeah. I bailed on him."

"Why now?"

"I don't know."

"You guilty fuck, Zeke. Twenty five years of fucking guilt. The great motivator."

"Easy pal, it sounds like you're getting a little riled. You're the one running away. Hiding out in this hovel."

"What the fuck do you know?"

"Hey don't lecture me, asshole. I heard the way you talked to that Billy Bum and his monkey-boy."

"Monkey-boy? Why did you call that kid a fucking monkey-boy?"

"That's what he looked like. A monkey. Why?"

"What, you think I hate them, that I despise them for what they are? Well, I don't. I hate the idea that my life has come to this. Working my way back to the primordial ooze. They're just reminders where I am. It's not personal. Those two get nothing but grief. They're here because they have nowhere else to go. Man, Zeke, you must have lived in a fucking gopher hole. It's what they have learned in this world, what the world has taught them. Yeah, you can blame them. But it's like giving kids constant access to violent video games and movies. They learn that violence is an option in resolving conflict. It's what we fucking teach them. Over and over and over until they get it. Then we wonder what happened in Columbine."

"How is it that you've got things figured out?"

"I don't. I'm still looking for meaning here, Zeke. Fucking answers. Like you!"

"I don't see a gun to your head."

"Look, you prick, I know we have choices in this life. But it's not everything. Viktor Frankl was a survivor of Auschwitz. He told the story of one cold morning when he was loaded into the back of a truck with other Jews bound for the concentration camps. There was this young German soldier guarding them with a rifle. He was cradling a cup of coffee. It was cold and he was shivering. A kid like him. He realized just then that he could have been that young soldier. Under similar circumstances. Leading innocent people to their deaths. What was that kid thinking?

"And when you grabbed me by the throat, there wasn't much difference between us. Fear is fear. As there isn't much difference between us right now. Who knows, I could have been a homosexual."

"Why would you want to be?"

Steven jumped up from his mattress. Fell forward on his knees. "I don't believe it, Zeke. You fucking homophobe. God save Saskatchewan!" He pulled the tarp back and slipped out into the dark and began to shout. Raged against the night.

"Billy Bum and the monkey-boy are fucking homos. They woke

up one day and said, 'let's be fags'. Come see Billy Bum and the monkey-boy in, The Don Valley Queers!" A wicked laugh, scornful and shrill.

John Trickett closed his eyes as the shouts rang harshly through his head. The spinning wouldn't stop. He was numb by the paradox that was Steven. He hated him. He hated the ravines and the desperation. The hopelessness that lurked about like shadows.

chapter
SIXTEEN

In the morning John Trickett opened his eyes and regretted stopping to help Sonny Merlot. Looked at his watch. Nearly noon. He hadn't slept that late in his entire life. Silhouettes of leaves laced the ceiling, swaying, scratching. Gashes of sunlight. He was covered with a blanket. He looked over at Steven, the explosion of hair from his quilt, the muffled dieseling of stale air. Wine bottles and Tim Horton's cups on the floor. The eternal watching of the African boy and ants arriving in single-file. Another party. Then someone lifting the front flap of the tarp. The big head of the ranting woman.

"Steven," she shrilled, "it's Sunday. Are you coming to the service?"

"He's sleeping," John Trickett said to the girl in a cranky tone. Hoped it would send her away. He tried to move but his back had seized. The cold damp cardboard. He threw off the blanket. He was fully dressed and still wearing his boots.

"Not for long," she said crawling into the shelter. She took hold of Steven's shoulders and began to shake him. "Steven, get up!"

Steven's arm came up swinging. "Fuck off, Angela," he said, "didn't you hear Zeke?

"Funny name. Zeke. Sounds like he should be raking leaves."

"Yeah, I'm just taking a break," John said. He had about enough of that nickname.

"Your fucking hilarious, Zeke," Steven said.

"What's his story?" Angela said tossing her head towards John.

"He came out from Saskatchewan to find his brother. Going to bring the Bug Man home. Save his crazy-assed soul."

"Good for you, Zeke." She nodded approvingly. Impressed with a good Christian. "Now, Steven," she said, "it's Sunday and you promised me that you would come to our service. Do a talk for the others."

"I was lying." His head still buried.

"Steven!"

"Shut up, Angela."

"You'll come then?"

"Yeah, later. Me and my partner here have business up near the Brick Works."

"Okay, later. It'll be an evening service. Bring Zeke, it looks like he needs some mothering." A parting look to John as she backed out of the shelter.

John managed to sit up. He was certain that he didn't need mothering. His hat was squashed and he beat it into shape. He sat miserably with a furry tongue and he was thirsty and filthy and thought about the hotel room. Slip out and get cleaned up. A good breakfast of bacon and eggs and toast with raspberry jam spread thick and sweet. Maybe some pancakes with maple syrup. Surely they had pancakes in Toronto. Coffee to smooth out his edges. Lots of coffee. He would come back in time for Steven to take him to Luke's camp. Save him a piece of bacon.

But he quickly realized the inequity in such thinking. He sat there and felt the hard reality of Steven's life. Thought of what he said the night before. Drinking wine and telling horrifying stories. Death in Africa. Then he remembered how Steven staggered out of the shelter. Something he said. Told the world about Billy Bum and the monkey-boy. He wondered what their names were. They had names. Of course they had names.

Steven sat up and noticed John Trickett looking at him with that wondering vigilance. "What?" he said.

"Didn't have to yell like that."

"Fucking Tarzan, eh?"

"Saw no need for it."

"It was your fault, Zeke."

"I don't think so."

"You hungry?"

"As hell."

Steven pulled out the styro-foam box and opened the lid. "Since you brought me half, I'll return the favour. Sound like a deal, Zeke?"

"No thanks."

"Suit yourself," Steven said. He crammed the leftover sandwich into his mouth then swung his legs over the edge of his mattress and pulled on his running shoes. "Let's go," he said, "sun is just about right. You'll want to see it when it's lit up. If we don't find your brother, it'll be worth the trip. Believe me."

"We'll find him."

Steven stared at him. Not hard. A look. "You're not such a bad old Zeke. You just haven't got out much. Kind of bushed, I would say."

"Is that a compliment?"

"An observation."

They stumbled out of the shelter and pissed back to back like duelists. Then John followed Steven out of the thick woods to the trail along the river. He walked stiff gaited like a circuit cowboy. He removed his hat and raked his hair with his fingers. Picked the sleep from the corners of his eyes. Dug out his ear wax and cleared his nostrils. Rough grooming. Made sure no one was looking. Made Steven stop and turn to him.

"What was that? Fuck, Zeke." Looked over his shoulder and down his back. That fierce farmer blow.

"I need a cup of coffee," John said.

"Yeah, me too. I think there's a Starbucks just past that tree." Rolled his eyes.

"I'll get a headache without it."

"I think I'm going to fucking cry." Put on a pouting look.

"Yeah, well, you're probably use to it."

"No, being hungry, dirty and feeling like shit everyday is not something you ever get use to. And I can hardly wait for fucking winter."

"I have a hard time believing that you want to live down here. And that you just can't say, fuck it, I'm going back home. Clean myself up - get a job - save some money - go back to school."

"Did you say, fuck it, Zeke?"

"Let's go, Steven. I need to get this done."

"Is that all I need to do? Damn. I wish I would have thought of that."

"All I'm saying is that your pretty bright for a lunatic."

"Now there's a compliment."

"No, just an observation."

They walked side by side along the river trail and met Sunday walkers who eyed them with suspicion, unworthy of any inference of a salutation. John felt their assumptions, that he too was reduced to a vagrant, a fringe dweller slouched and wanting. It wasn't too difficult to pick out the visitors. Hair tamed to some modern style and clothes clean and matching and a certain purpose to their movements. That willful swagger. Cameras to record their scheduled leisure and cell phones pressed to tilted heads. The plump and florid images of mainstream masking some other wanting. John was beginning to think that everyone had it in varying degrees. Something human that rises from no dearth of troubles.

They crossed under the racket of the Bloor Street Viaduct. The sun was hot on John Trickett's back and his neck was sticky with sweat. He wouldn't take off his jean jacket as he liked to have his hands free and he suffered because of it. But he would never consider complaining about his discomforts other than craving for coffee. His head began to ache dully from caffeine withdrawal. It was bothersome but he tolerated it.

"You never answered me, Steven," John said to keep his brain distracted.

"I'll walk out of here one day, Zeke. Don't worry about me."

"I'm not."

"Just save your fucking brother."

"Yeah. How far now?"

"Just look for it below that bluff. You'll see the light."

"I don't see anything."

"You will."

"What did Angela mean by mothering?"

"I think she thought you were a sad sack of shit and in need of some attention. Either that or she has a crush on you."

"You sure can be an asshole. Give me a smoke"

"Get your own."

"Fucking unbelievable."

"You're starting to swear a lot, Zeke."

"You're a bad influence."

"You can never be sure what is good or bad. It's a matter of perspective. Points of view. Things just are. Nothing black and white. I saw this bumper sticker once when I was working Queen Street and it read: Auntie Em, hate you. Hate Kansas. Taking the dog. Dorothy."

"That's pretty funny."

"Are you going to laugh?"

"What are you going to talk about at that service? Doesn't seem proper with your mouth. Fuck this. Fuck that."

"Well, it's my father. He still has hope for me. He's trying to lure me back to St. Andrews. His Don Valley congregation. He gave Angela something for me to read to the addicts. I think he hopes I have an epiphany or something."

"A what?"

"You know. The lightning bolt. I suddenly will have everything figured out."

"Yeah, isn't that what I said?"

"It's a little different, Zeke, than saying fuck it."

"Anyway, it doesn't look like he's about to quit on you. That's something."

"Yeah."

The way Steven looked at him just then. The way their eyes met. Some understanding. John Trickett had the impression that Steven somehow liked him. Perhaps admired him. Steven seemed to enjoy their banter, that same talk John had found offensive. There was nothing offensive about it really. That was just a veneer. Steven was more than cussing and sarcasm and had a odd sense of humour. It leaked through when John tried not to take his raillery personally.

The valley veered and something flashed. There was little doubt what it was. Shafts of diaphanous light bore out of the hardwoods like searchlight beams where a ravine cleft deep into the bluffs of the Don.

"This is the spot," Steven said. "Most people think nothing of it. They think it's a window from a house up on the ridge. A piece of broken glass. Something explainable. Not so amazing."

"Isn't that something?" John said removing his hat like a rancher beholden.

"You're so melodramatic, Zeke."

"It seems to be changing. Moving. Like the northern lights."

"Come on, let's see it up close before it's gone. It doesn't last long. It's like a sunset."

John's heart beat quickened as he followed Steven. His eyes peering into the shadowed woods expecting to see someone darting from tree to tree. A phantom among them. Luke stealing along the fringes, watching, speculating in his distorted mind what it was that drew him to that man who called out to him where cars delivered his booty of bugs. What remote memory was sparking and whispering, arcing through the static of years? Some truth lost to him.

But there was nothing there along the unmarked path that left the Belt Line Trail save for the flash of juncos and a fat grey squirrel watching inverted and stiff from the trunk of a maple. Its jerky descent. Tentative. And then the sunless woods brightened, the transition from night into day. And as John Trickett broke from the shrouded woodland into a luminous clearing, Steven was already standing slack and agape before an abstract scene alien contrived. That scene in the dark woods from ET. A space ship made out of jars.

chapter
SEVENTEEN

"He's not here," Steven said, his head slowly turning to take in the Bug Man's lair. A mechanical rotation. Then a flash of movement. Form slipping through the trees.

John saw it too and rushed forward. "Luke!" he called out. "Luke Trickett, it's me John. Come back. It's your brother Johnny!" Then stillness. His panting breath. The jars. His mind skeptical of what his eyes could see.

"He shot out of here like a fucking arrow," Steven said. "I told you he's a hard fucker to catch."

"We can wait. He heard his name. He'll remember. He'll be back."

"Alright. You sound sure, Zeke."

"You don't have to stay."

"There's no way I want to miss this reunion."

"It might be a while."

"Like I've got somewhere to go."

"What about Angela?"

"If you can bring your brother in, I'll have something to talk about. They just might start to bawl. Inspire them to quit this place. Inspire me, Zeke, You never know."

They stood shoulder to shoulder like travelers to a lost world of myth and fantasy. Before them a glass menagerie, shimmering, effulgent, alive with shadowed insects clicking in jars and suspended dead in amber fluids, jars of every size and shape, walls of glass fired by the sun, a labyrinth of jars, a maze so astounding in planning and art that it seemed all at once some tribe's reckoning of the world when the passing of seasons was tracked by ancient physics. A camp, a palace shaped out of jars. Geometry of some unknown significance. Some purpose to the creator, craftsman, artisan, madman. Luke.

Slowly they moved around the periphery, walls as high as John could reach, the light splayed, mirrored and scattered into a thousand diamonds. Reflected, refracted. Prisms fanned out, disappeared, reappeared. Blinding. Electric. And struck by such intensity of light, John turned to the shadows inside the jars, the insects that he knew, that he would never forget. He pressed in close, but Steven stayed back, cautious of the ugliness, the revolting collection, unmoving. For they were dead, a host in each jar. But still the clicking from somewhere near. Dragonflies, Green Darners and Ten Spots, their great wings outstretched, plucked from the hard combs of radiators. Rows of them. Fat black nymphs, worms and caterpillars bloated in fluid. Preserved. Magnified. Crickets and Cicadas. Giant Water Bugs like turtles. Hercules Beetles, Ox Beetles, Stag Beetles in shiny black armour, mandibles like antlers. And sinister Mantises still praying in death. Row on row like cells of some grand collector. A tribute to Class Insecta. The paranoid projection of Luke's hallucinations, his highly organized imaginary world made real.

And John entered the glass fortress through a portal, a threshold facing west and another facing east, a way in and a way out. Steven followed. They crept like pirates, their careful footfall as there on the floor wooden pallets duly bristled with pinned insects, a forest of dead hulls tagged with identification. John knelt down to read the inscriptions, but they were illegible. It was the same way that Luke collected insects as a boy. Pinned through the thorax and labeled. Coleoptera, Carrion Beetle. Luke Trickett, Collector. Battle Creek

Sask., August 19, 1972.

A narrow isle between the pallets of impaled bugs lead to a stack of pallets covered with blankets. Some shrine to the insect gods. A gas lantern on a makeshift table. The lure of light in the pitch black Don. In the corner the entomologist tool kit: wide-mouthed jars with rubber stoppers, tape, jars of ethyl alcohol, a net, nail polish, a jar of potassium cyanide, a tin of fumigent, cotton balls, hand lens, tin of No.1 insect pins. And still the clicking.

On the opposite end of the enclosure boxes with clear plastic covers pulled taught and taped. Holes poked through for ventilation. John and Steven peered over the sides into the box of incessant clicks. Countless black beetles with eyes on the back of their heads. Click Beetles, many on their backs, flipping into the air with a loud click to right themselves. Pelting rain on a tin roof. Then another box, open, with twigs and leaves. Black pupae, green and gold chrysalises. Chubby yellow caterpillars like miniscule school buses. Butterflies emerging, splitting their metamorphic chambers: Tiger Swallowtail, Red Admiral, Mourning Cloak. Unfurling. Pumping their life fluids into wrinkled wings. Friable as rice paper. Another box with great eyed moths with antennae like feathered quill pens. Sphinx Moth, Silk Moth and a striking Luna Moth in a delicate green cape with sweeping tails.

"Let's get out of here, Zeke. This place is fucking creepy."

"I couldn't have imagined this."

"Yeah, what was he thinking?"

"He was thinking about bugs. Just bugs."

Butterflies began to take flight. The inaugural lift off, flitting all about them. They seemed confused by the light at first as they reckoned with the renovations to their bodies, but soon lifted above the jars and began to circle. Rising higher and higher like birthday balloons. And beyond the canopy, grasses and wetlands of the free world.

John Trickett hauled a section of a broken pallet to the easterly approach and sat down to wait for Luke to return. There was a good part of the day left. The sun dipped and the radiance about them dimmed. Someone shut off the light. The glass encampment seemed to lose its magic. A discordant collection of jars stacked like poor brick work. Leaning and propped with tree branches, chinked with moss and clods of mud. Jars with labels clearly visible. Peanut butter and pickles and mayonnaise.

"And City Hall wonders why recycling is down in Cabbagetown," Steven said. "Every fucking jar and cockroach in Toronto is here."

John turned to Steven. Close to a laugh.

"You want me to shut the fuck up, Zeke?" That satirical grin.

"I would appreciate it," John said, "if you just sit quiet." He was getting used to Steven, to the way he talked. His frank manner. Harley Buck with an attitude. Sitting there he looked down at his hands. They were dirty. As were his jeans and jean jacket. He rubbed his chin whiskers and ran his tongue over his teeth and spat. He was hungry. He turned to Steven again. There wasn't much difference between them. He supposed that anyone who came along wouldn't be able to guess which one of them was the rancher. Identification with a way of life or vocation didn't make much sense. There in the Don labels weren't useful. Just men trying to find their way and women too, like the crusading Angela, trying to help those the world forgot. Sinners all, unknown at Toronto's doorstep. And Africa, so far away, how could it ever be imagined, confirmed? As if to accept the genocide, recognize the brutality, look into the face of horror, would turn a man's heart into stone. Steven chiseling away with his fulminations and Luke out there in the woods.

So close now. It did not seem possible that it could be Luke, his brother who he loved, shared the mysteries of Windrush, Luke in the picture that he kept in his pocket. And as John thought of these things, a stampede of images in his head, he glimpsed Nora's fear. He could understand her despair over his decision to leave. His promise to his mother. It all seemed so outrageous now. Harley was right of course. The good Doctor.

They sat there until their sore asses roused them from the pallet to stand and stretch. John moved towards the woods, down a slight grade, peering. Something that wasn't there before. A shadow standing.

"See something?" Steven said. He stood alongside John, attentive, their breaths drawn and checked.

"There, beside that tree," John whispered. Arm raising slowly to point. No abrupt movement.

"Yeah, I see him. It's the Bug Man. He's just standing there. Call him."

"No. Give him time."

Motionless, they waited. And finally the Bug Man stepped towards them, the sun striking the lower part of his leg. But still a dark apparition, formless. As if only a part of him had stepped into present reality and the rest of him remained in the realm of fables. John did wish to call out to him, but if he did Luke might flee once again. So shy he was, like a rare species on the brink of discovery. Extinction. Then the Bug Man moved forward, one foot then the other, impossibly slow, cautious. A movie, frame by frame.

Then John spoke at last. "Luke," he said, "it's okay. I'm here to help you. I'm here to take you home."

And the Bug Man came closer, painted by the sun from his shoulders to his miserable shoes. Closer still and finally he emerged from his vague existence into a pool of light as if teleported. Beamed down. His eyes welded to John, eyes peering out of his thatch of hair and beard. Manson eyes. So close now that John was certain he was meeting his brother for the first time in twenty five years. Under that ruination and tatters was Luke Trickett. And John's fear and guilt and repulsion, his weakness, the abandonment made real under the queer scrutiny of his brother. There is no help for Luke, his mother said over and over. He could hear her now. 'He is sick, Johnny, and can never be helped. Forget about him. Forget that he ever lived.

He'll never know that he had a family. He'll soon forget when the sickness gets bad. It is better this way, Johnny. Forget Luke. There is no cure for his sickness. It is best for everyone. No long faces now. Luke is gone.'

Those words long buried. He believed them. Had to believe them. And his father would slip away into the barn to the bottle of rye he kept there. Fend off his culpability. It all began to come back as he stood there. Guilty on all counts. And his mother watching her brother Tommy hanging from his neck. Alone in the house. The smell of drying shit. His blue death mask.

And John thought that he might reach out with his hand. Touch him. Hold on to him so that he could never run away. "That's it, Luke," he said, his hand opening. An invitation to recovery. A redeeming hand. But there was no rush of feeling, nor absolution. No unmistakable connection. Nothing remote to the exhilaration of reunion.

Then Luke's eyes shifted away from him. Alarmed. And before John could turn to see what it was that startled him so, an explosion bore out of the silence and concussed the side of his head, the shock waves of close range gunshot. Steven vaulted forward and Luke sprawled on the ground holding his stomach. John spun on his heels, crouching, and there slumped against the jar wall was the monkey-boy with a handgun shivering in his hand like a fish, his face all twisted in a vengeful grimace and sobbing with great dreadful gulps.

And he lowered the gun to Steven who had not moved but lay with his face pushed into the dirt and an arm caught under him and blood showing on his back, spreading darkly. Radially. And John deafened by the blast and stunned by the sudden collapse of Steven and Luke. The blood on Steven's back and Luke emitting painful whimpers like a car-hit dog. Shot they were, real and wounded or dead.

John raised his hand to the monkey-boy. "No!" he pleaded as he dropped to his knees. But the gun was armed and deadly and the monkey-boy took aim on him now, determined to shoot again. And John glanced to Luke who moved still, disabled by the shot but no blood about his ragged clothes. All was lost it seemed to him, his journey a tragic mistake. So present he was with his fear, he could feel it, a pervading field, a palpable hopelessness. Unable to defend himself or Luke and Steven dying. Waiting for the bullet. The feel of it tearing into his flesh. Splintered bones. Killed there in the humid vaults of the Don River. The eternal echo. And the receding imagery of Saskatchewan, a past life where he had a family, their names and faces fading like old photographs.

The monkey-boy returned to Steven, to shoot him again. As if steadied by murderous recollection. And then Billy Bum emerged breathless from the glass portal and began to scream at his companion at once as if he already knew what he would find. "What have you done?" He stood there with his arms stiff and shaking, panicked by the sight of Steven prone and bloodied and still. Some other fetal construct of a man, obscure, heaped in pain.

And John Trickett, frozen in his crouch lest he be shot himself, saw advantage in Billy's arrival. "He didn't hate you," he said coolly looking right into the monkey-boy's eyes. As if the truth would be reaffirmed there. "He didn't hate you at all. It wasn't about you. Billy, stop him."

And Billy lunged for the monkey-boy's arm and pushed it away and the gun discharged and struck the glass wall and shattered the jars and the wall collapsed. Then another and another and like dominoes the jars came down and all manner of insects dead and alive scattered among the shards. Then Billy pulled the monkey-boy away and they disappeared into the woods.

Stillness fell upon John Trickett, a dark smothering of hopelessness. And still Steven hadn't moved. Dead it seemed. And he scrambled to Luke and tore at his rags to find his wound. Pulled his hands away, the bloodied fingers. He managed to lift the layers of clothing, a hole through each one and a ragged hole in his belly, black and seeping. He felt his back and no blood showed on his fingers. The bullet that went through Steven was still in him. He removed his jean jacket and ripped his shirt sleeve off and packed it against Luke's wound. "Hold it, Luke. Hold it against your gut." And instinctively Luke did so.

And John turned back to Steven and took hold of his shoulder and lifted his head from the dirt. He held him against his knee and cleaned the dirt from his nose and mouth. Then he held him away from himself to look at his wound, felt the wet blood, the tack of it and lifted his shirt, and there an exit wound like a saucer below his ribs that frothed and sucked. "Oh, no," he said.

And Steven's eyes moved and his lips parted to speak. "That fucking homo, eh, Zeke," he said. Blood showing on his lips.

"Shut up," John said. "Just shut the fuck up."

"Sure." A trailing out-breath, lost.

John covered him with his jean jacket and behind him the springing of click beetles and the last of the jars toppled. A flaw in the fabric of his world.

chapter
EIGHTEEN

In the back of the police car John Trickett could see himself running through the woods frantic for help. And those visitors to the Don, strolling the Belt Line Trail, recoiling and turning away, hurrying their children from the wild eyed ravine dweller who emerged from the shadows with bloodied hands and ripped shirt, all animate and wet with the gore of his victims. And how they heard the shots and called the Toronto Police and called again as the shooter seemed crazed and desperate among them.

The police were wary and skeptical and forced him to the ground. He spat out his story like machine gun fire and took them to the scene. His identity was confirmed and he repeated over and over that Luke was his brother and had schizophrenia. He would be allowed to go to the hospital before being escorted to the Toronto Police Station. Further confirmation and a formal statement. More questions. The name of the monkey-boy. Tragic on all accounts.

The police car followed the ambulance to the Toronto General Hospital and John was ushered into the Emergency ward and told to stay in the waiting room. But he didn't care to be idle and soon wandered down the hall and there through a window discovered Steven and Luke lying on gurneys side by side. But there were no doctors attending Steven. His clothes stripped off him and a blue sheet across his midriff. His wound covered with wads of bloody packing. And doctors and nurses surrounded Luke with scissors cutting away at his clothing, the rotting layers like humus, dark and organic.

A nurse held a garbage bag as the foul veneers were dropped into it and they glanced to one another at the mystery there before them. This man who lived in the shadowed fringes of Toronto. The Bug Man. And they peeled the rags from Luke like an onion. Down to the last layer. A dirty grey hide and beneath, festered sores and boils caked and fused to rancid cotton. They pulled and a piece of flesh ripped away. Then the nurses dampened the cloth and sores with sponges and cut away the remnants leaving a patchwork upon him. And the doctor attended to the bullet wound, poked and prodded. Listened to his heart. An intravenous drip into his arm. And the last of the clothing removed, a skinny, milk-white, pockmarked body was all that remained of Luke. A species of wild-man driven out of the woods, shot to vanquish the fear of such monsters that lurk just out of the field of compassion. Monsters killing monsters. Men killing men.

Luke was moved to the intensive care unit and John sat in the family lounge to search in his mind for the purpose of his coming, what had brought him to that place in time. Deep thoughts for a man who perceived life through dust and squeals of castration and the chaff of harvest. A doctor walked into the lounge with a police officer. Pale green scrubs and a surgical mask around his neck. Like a jockstrap.

"John Trickett," he said.

"Yeah." John stood up and wiped his hands on his jeans to prepare for a handshake. But the doctor knew better.

"Mr. Trickett, your brother is stable," the doctor said. "We're trying to get copies of his records from British Columbia. It will be a challenge now that the institution where he resided is no longer in operation. We'll need to assess him to determine the best course of treatment. He's extremely malnourished and dehydrated. You might want to wait a day or two before you come back. He has a lot of lesions that are infected. He has scars on his arms from drug use and what appears to be from self-harm. Perhaps suicide attempts. He's very ill. His weight is under 90 pounds."

"Thanks, Doctor. I appreciate all you can do for him."

"It's an astonishing situation, Mr. Trickett. Right here in Toronto. We have all heard stories of the Bug Man. A local legend. Something out of Tolkien."

John nodded. His hands in his pockets. It seemed just then an unseemly story. Suitable for tabloids at supermarket checkouts. Rancher from Saskatchewan captures Big Foot.

"What about the other one?" he said. "Steven."

The doctor's head dropped slightly. The grace of sensitive men. "His wounds were critical," he said. "His life signs were weak. He lost most of his blood volume. He died soon after he was brought in. There was nothing more that we could do for him."

"I can't believe he's dead."

"It's never easy when life ends so young."

"I don't even know his last name. His father is an elder at St. Andrews. That's all I know. Someone should tell him."

"The Toronto Police will look after that, Mr. Trickett," the doctor said. He reached out and touched John's shoulder. Let his hand rest there for several seconds. Consoling. Then he turned and hurried down the long hall and disappeared through the split of double doors.

The police officer stood to one side and John sat back down. Exhausted.

"Just a few minutes, Mr. Trickett," the police officer said.

"I'm ready to go," John said. He leaned forward to stand up but he couldn't. Cupped his face with his great hands. Weary. The smell of dried blood. Then all at once he felt a trembling from within him. It came from deep down, a surge, everything that he had buried there, the unacquainted parts of himself, failures and regrets, wounds never healed, and guilt, the weighty slug of it, all rising now. And there was not a thing for him to do. No resistence. He didn't care. Bring it on.

And he cried there in that chair and the police officer stepped outside into the hallway. It wasn't fear of losing Luke that tapped the underground river nor was it the dreadful sight of him. The bones of his hips and pelvis like a sun-bleached saddle. His incomprehensible ambition to bring Luke home. He had no feeling towards Luke as he lay there. Nothing. No outpouring of love and compassion. It wasn't Luke at all, but Steven. And how he hated him those first days along the Don River. And now he cried for him. The sadness of an incomplete life. A misunderstood soul betrayed by the world he wished to help. Something inside him that John recognized as good, a quality of wisdom that broke through his personality. Light leaking through blinds shut to the world. A split in his contemptible rind.

John wiped his eyes with the back of his hands. Passed a knuckle under his nose as a photographer stopped at the door. Someone else with him, hidden.

"John Trickett?" he said.

John nodded to the photographer and the camera flashed. The photographer turned away and Alex Grove was left standing there. Sheepish. Back on the story. The dramatic conclusion.

"I thought you were doing travel," John said.

"The story of the Bug Man just got interesting," Alex said.

"Interesting?"

"What would you call it?"

"I don't know. A mistake?" He looked at her. Waiting. "You're not writing this down."

"No, the press conference is over. I think I've got it all."

"You don't think it was a mistake my coming out here, somewhere I don't belong?"

"You came out here to save your brother, to get him out of the ravines. And you did that. All the obstacles along the way. Do you still have his picture? I would like to use it."

"You want to do a story about Luke?"

"The Bug Man. It's an astonishing story, Mr. Trickett."

"So I hear."

"People will want to hear this. They will want to read about your story, how you came from Saskatchewan to rescue your long lost brother. It's a feel-good story. God knows we need that these days."

"What about Steven? What about his story? He died. He was murdered by some frightened kid. What about his story?"

"It's true, they have stories. But they don't have the appeal of the Bug Man. Tragedy with a happy ending."

"Call him Luke. He's not the fucking Bug Man. I'm sick of that shit. Did you know that Steven was a medical student and went to Rwanda in 1994? An unbelievable slaughter. Hacked and mutilated. People. He went there to help and came back broken. That's the story, Ms. Grove. That's the story to tell. Not the story of my brother I left for dead in an institution. Don't celebrate his rescue like I'm some fucking hero. That's bullshit. I'm no hero."

He sat back and closed his eyes and shook. Emotion rippling through him. Aware that he swore in front of a woman. And the turn of things.

chapter
NINETEEN

John sat on the bed looking out the window. Haze over Toronto. It was going to be a hot one. Showered and shaved and nothing on except his underwear.

"Nora, it's me."

"John, what happened? My God!"

"You know?"

"It's on the news and in the paper. *Bug Man Revealed: Saskatchewan rancher John Trickett rescues brother lost in the Don River ravines for 25 years...!*"

"Calm down, Nora."

"Calm down? There's nothing to be calm about. If you want to know, Harley came flying up the driveway not twenty minutes ago. Skidding across the lawn. He burst right into the kitchen. Didn't even knock. Do you know how excited Harley needs to be to do that?"

"Yeah, I do."

"And he was shot. And another man killed. Were you there, John?"

"My ears are still ringing from that shot."

"Your picture in the paper. It looks like you were in a fight. What were you thinking?"

"It sounds worse than it was."

"Have you seen the paper? The Mayor wants an investigation. He was horrified that that could happen in Toronto?"

"No, I don't want to leave my room quite yet. I think there's reporters waiting in the lobby. I can see news vans out on the street. Who wrote the article?"

"It says, Alexandra Grove."

"Did she say anything about Steven?"

"Just that a homeless man was killed."

"Nothing about him?"

"Why?"

"I don't know. I just can't stop thinking about him."

"Just you, John."

"A lot of hero crap?"

"Yeah, John Trickett, hero. The simple rancher from Maple Creek."

"You sound like you don't approve."

"It's not that."

"You haven't asked about Luke."

Silence. The twisting of the phone cord. "How is he?"

"He's going to be alright. The bullet didn't hit any major organs. They're going to move him to Regina when the doctors get his medication sorted out. He'll likely be there a month before I can bring him home. Just a day at a time to begin with." Boldly stated. Assertive. He knew that Luke had a long road ahead of him. Doctors wouldn't allow him to leave unless he was able. He felt his wickedness and he reproached himself. Stood up with the telephone and moved to the window. Shaking his head.

Thicker silence. Like a black wall.

"How's my dad?"

"If you don't get back soon we'll be burying him without you." The return volley.

"I'll be home. How's my mother?"

"She didn't know who I was the last time I visited. Mumbling things about her brother Tommy. Swinging. Swinging. I won't go back."

And she didn't know about his Uncle Tommy. "Nora," John said.

"Yes."

"I understand."

"What is it that you understand, John?"

"Well, I don't know. How you feel, I guess."

In the background the kitchen door slammed. Mitch and Del stomping to dust off their boots. John could hear them talking to their mother. "Your father," she said to them. Strangers in a far away land, that was his home. Sons he didn't know. A wife that knew everything.

"I'll call you when I'm leaving," John said. Had to end it as always.

"That's fine."

"Alright." He had the urge to hurl the phone against the wall, but managed to resist it and sat back down on the bed. Collapsed. His head down between his legs like he was about to vomit. Elbows on his knees and his thumbs jammed into his bony eye sockets. Had enough of hotel living. Felt the call of the open road. But the anticipation of Windrush was sullied by his conversation with Nora, the cold silence that was not his silence this time, but hers alone that still opposed Luke's coming home, Luke's presence at Windrush all those years. And what now? The turn of summer was approaching, the sun eclipsing, passing from darkness into light again. The realization of his dream. To make all things right. With or without her. But he was getting ahead of himself. His mind leading the charge. Always defending. He hadn't seen Luke since he was brought in and there was something he needed to do before he went back to the hospital.

He looked up St. Andrews in the phone book and called the number. Said he was John Trickett and needed to speak to Steven's father. The woman in the office said his name was Mr. Sullivan. John made an appointment to meet with him. He put on a clean denim shirt and jeans and combed his hair. Wiped his boots with a hotel face cloth. Placed his Wheat Pool hat and bloodied clothes in a plastic bag and dumped it in the trash and stood there and looked down at it. Luke's and Steven's blood. The thought of leaving it there unsettled him. Something unclean and improper. Should be burned. So he took the bag and left the room and went down the elevator to the lobby. Settle his bill and face whoever might be waiting for him to appear. Could see no other away around it.

It had been an expensive stay in Toronto. And as the clerk behind the counter ran his credit card through, John Trickett didn't flinch at the total. It didn't seem to matter compared to the cost of a life and the suffering he had seen. But when the bills came in he would hear about it. The mere thought of it made his heart race and set his mind to defend his expenses. Nora hadn't even mentioned the state of his expenditures and yet he carried on the conversation in his mind as if she had done so. He was quick to anger over things that involved Luke. But he was beginning to understand that it didn't mount out of a sense of familial duty, rather a reflection of his frustration and his liability. He had conspired with everyone else to create the Bug Man.

The clerk gave him directions to St. Andrews. Then the shuffle of feet behind him. Ambush. He turned to a troop of faces, strange and eager. Alexandra Grove not among them. Cameras with microphones like readied missiles. Tape recorders raised to capture his words. A salvo of questions.

"Mr. Trickett, how does it feel to have found your brother?"

"Is it true that you lived in the ravines to help you find him?"

"What are your plans now? When will he go home? What is his condition?"

"What do you know about the suspect who shot your brother?"

"What is the status of the Don River people? How many homeless?"

"How does it feel to be a hero?"

All attention directed to him. His answers. What bits of wisdom and insights might trickle from his lips to inspire their stories, articles, clips? The word hero elicited a remote pleasure. A vague but seductive feeling that stood opposed to what he knew was true. They all wanted to hear what Alex Grove championed, his noble journey into the despairing shadow lands of the Don to rescue the hapless victim of an insane world. A light among them. And how easily it would be to weave the path of triumph, how he seized the sword of virtue and hacked through the thorny woods to face the gnashing teeth of darkness. And how he teetered there. A temptation that began to swell. As if his thoughts fed it, gave some truth to it, allowed it to breathe in him. Be him. And then a question awoke him from his dream.

"Why was Steven Sullivan with you?"

"Sullivan?"

"Steven Sullivan, the other shooting victim."

How odd, the sound of Steven's full name seemed to restore his humanity, reconnect him with a history of people. Sullivan's stretching back into the past, a chain now broken. So many questions probing a rancher's mind to its depths. But still John didn't know how to answer. What to say about him. A complexity beyond his acumen. "Please, I need to go," he said.

"What do you know about Steven Sullivan, Mr. Trickett?" They sensed something more.

"I don't know!" John said losing his patience, his opportunity. He left them all standing in the lobby with nothing but the certainty of his pastoral reserve. Punish the bastards with silence.

Another parkade in the heart of Toronto. And there along King Street St. Andrews reflected in a glass high-rise. The CN tower looming above in the background. John Trickett turned and there it was, huddled ancient and salient between the contemporary attributes of the city. He crossed King Street at Simcoe and stood before it, the twin towers and arched entrance. Something of indestructible granite to outlive them all. A stillness amid the mad rush.

He silently hoped that it was locked, but the great heavy door groaned open and he stepped tentatively into the dark cavern of the church. Some holy place that was strange to him. In the interior chancel a long row of pews. Brilliant stained glass windows. Decorated ceiling above the alter. Pillars. A place of worship. And there in the front row a figure bowed in prayer. He thought he might be intruding so he stood there in the aisle unwilling to move forward. He looked away to see if there might be someone who could assist him. And when he turned back the figure in the pew was standing in the aisle facing him. A thin middle-aged man with an odd perceptive tilt to his head. It startled him and he felt himself jump.

"Angela said that you were a friend of Steven's," the man said. A sad weak voice. His hands clasped behind him.

"Mr. Sullivan?"

"Yes, Mr. Trickett."

"You know who I am."

"You just called, didn't you?" A smile. Heavy eyes.

"Yeah, I'm not thinking too good."

"I've seen your picture in the paper. You were with Steven."

"I'm sorry, sir."

"I feared such a thing, Mr. Trickett. I prayed that it wouldn't come to that. Pleaded with him to leave the ravines."

"I think he was going to leave," John said. "He said so. I came here to tell you that."

Mr. Sullivan nodded ever so slightly. An impression. A grim smile. He brought his hands forward holding a book.

"Come," he said drawing his hand toward him as if he wished to dispense his wisdom. The way of elders.

John Trickett did so. He wondered if he might have to endure a selection of scripture.

Mr. Sullivan opened the book. "Steven was partial to this book. I think it would be proper if you would have it. Pass it on. *Man's Search for Meaning*. I don't know that he found it. Perhaps it will be helpful to you. I don't know. One has to have faith that meaning lies beneath our anguish. Without meaning, I think we would lose hope."

"Yes, sir. Thank you."

"Do you have a particular faith, Mr. Trickett?"

"I suppose not."

"It doesn't matter." His head dropped. Resigned

"Are you alright, Mr. Sullivan?"

"Oh, I confess that I struggle with the meaning of this. The why? Such promise and future and all the possibilities of life. So young. How can I reconcile this? I pray to God for meaning. Answers. But all I can hear is the desolate silence. His life no longer rings in my ears. The hope that he would leave that place, reclaim himself, rise from the ashes like the Pheonix. I will remain here, Mr. Trickett, until I hear the answer. The meaning of his death."

"I wouldn't have found my brother without him. That's something."

"Yes."

John Trickett accepted the book and ran his hand over the cover. As if some message in braille was inscribed there. "I wonder why my brother Luke had to live the way he did for twenty five years. He was sick and alone. I could have done something long ago. I can't imagine there's meaning for that."

"We search, Mr. Trickett. That is our nature. The story of our lives. Today, or perhaps in the end we will know. When we stand before God."

"I was hoping to find it here in Toronto. Before I leave."

"Toronto is a place in time. To remain here is to remain in the present moment. To listen. It is not a place. Wherever we are, we are here."

"Yeah," John said. The way he did when talk turned deep and thoughtful. Then the stillness around him. Awkward. Figures in stained-glass leaning towards him. Judging. He began to back away, a sure sign that his business in the church was done. But he stopped himself and caught the flame of red slash across his chest from the glass. "I'm no hero," he confessed.

Mr. Sullivan nodded. A suggestion for further testimony. "What is a hero?" he said.

John Trickett pulled at his chin. "A man to be admired, I imagine," he said.

"You are admired, are you not?"

"The media is making me out to be something I'm not. To sell papers."

"It is a point of view. It doesn't make it real. Do you know what is real, Mr. Trickett?"

"I do, sir."

"Then what can be done?"

"I think they need to hear the truth. Steven deserves that much. He was honest about things and people should know that. Not just that he was killed. I don't know that he would agree to it, but it seems to me the right thing to do."

Mr. Sullivan did not answer. He stood there like a stone likeness of himself. In the dull church light the subtle details of expression were not discernable. Then after a time he clasped his hands behind his back and turned away and returned to his posture in the front row of pews.

chapter
TWENTY

In a room in the Intensive Care Unit a nurse in a pink uniform stood vigilant over Luke like a bottle of Pepto-Bismol. John washed his hands at a sink with a sign warning of the transmission of germs through touch. He imagined the germs that Luke hosted down along the Don River bottomland. At home in his clothes and encampment. Bugs of all sizes.

"Your brother is awake, Mr. Trickett," the nurse said. "He is beginning to respond to his medication. But he's been unmedicated for such a long time, we don't know which drug will be most effective. We'll use trial and error. It will be a long way back for him."

"You started anti-psychotics?"

"Yes. So just a few minutes with him and don't expect too much."

"Thanks," John said. The nurse stepped back and allowed him to sit at Luke's bedside.

There he was, Luke Trickett. His hair cut and face shaven, though stubble had already grown back along his jaw line. Silver tinged. He stared up at the ceiling. Monitors around him with graphic displays, digital outputs, blood pressure and blood gas, clear plastic bags on hooks that dripped intravenous and tubes taped to his skin. Temples wired. He wore a thin blue gown that didn't cover his scant shoulders. White bone and bandaged sores. He lay perfectly straight. A tremor in his hand.

John leaned over the bed. "Luke," he said, "it's John. Everything is going to be alright now."

John held Luke's hand that stuck out from under the bed sheets. Fingertips raw from the scrubbing. He studied those blue eyes that looked up like a dull day. Life squeezed out of them, colour leached and lost but responsive to the sound of his voice. Luke turned to him slow and listless. His eyes wandered over John's face, inch by inch as if mapping recollection, feeding the memory traces of his brain to validate what he saw there before him. Then back to the ceiling. Awareness or perhaps base neurological impulses.

Then John's silent voice. It is Luke, but a stranger. He doesn't know me. Then will I walk away like before? What makes me persevere? Is it Nora, to show her, to face her, to stand up to her? Why can't I cry for him?

Then a doctor on his rounds. "Mr. Trickett." Everyone knew him. The story.

"Yes." Shaken out of his self-scrutiny.

"I understand you wish to have your brother brought home."

"Yeah."

"We will do what we can to transport him to Regina. But we will be unable to do that until we determine a course of treatment. He has been on his own a long time."

"Twenty five years in the ravines."

"Now that's something we just don't know. The mentally ill who live on the street tend to move around. In and out of crisis centres. On and off of medication. We have no way of knowing if he can return to a relatively stable life. He will need intensive psychotherapy. Counseling. There is much uncertainty here, Mr. Trickett. You must know this. I'm not trying to alarm you. Your family will be paramount in his treatment. Family support is critical."

John nodded. His failing. What family? "He has family support."

"Very good. That is everything."

"Yeah."

"How long are you in town?"

"I should go soon."

"There's not much for you to do right now. We'll make arrangements when your brother improves enough to be moved. You'll be contacted."

"Alright. I wasn't sure if I should leave."

The doctors fleeting smile as he turned away. A swift recognition of something. Admiration or a glimpse of his faltering.

He sat on a bench outside the hospital on University Avenue and leaned back with his face to the sun and closed his eyes. Weary as he had ever been. He imagined finding a place to live and vanishing from the world. Then he thought he heard a calf bawling. A rancher's equivalent to ringing in the ears. But it was some old busker's horn ensemble. Then he found himself sitting in someone's shade.

"How is he?" Alexandra Grove said. Two cups of Starbuck's coffee in her hand.

"Fine." Brought his hand up to his brow like a salute.

"Something a child would say, John."

"I didn't think you were that interested in Luke. Just the story."

"Yeah, well screw that. That's not why I'm here."

"Sit down," John said sliding over. Took the coffee and thanked her.

"Look, I'm sorry. I feel awful about it. I know it wasn't what you wanted."

"I don't feel like a hero, you know. Maybe for a minute. But it didn't last. Only the truth lasts. Bullshit is usually a short term affair. No substance. Just smell."

"Did you make that up?"

"No, I can't take credit for that either. It comes from a famous Saskatchewan philosopher. Harley Buck. Sage of the short grass. Something like that."

She didn't laugh. "I guess you had to be there."

"Yeah."

"It's old news now. I can't retract it. My editor had me emphasize certain aspects of my piece. But I'm not going to sit here and blame him. It was my story. My name. I thought it was good. Hey, I'm sorry. I wish there was something I could do for you."

"Well, there is."

"What's that?"

"You can go down to St. Andrews and speak to Steven Sullivan's father. He's an elder there. Ask him about Steven. His dreams. Africa. How he set out to help heal the world only to be sucked into a black hole. And how he tried to climb out. Tell that story and we're even. That's what you can do."

She sat there and nodded. Looking into the squint of a rancher's eyes. Considering what it would take. The creative possibilities.

"Alright, I can do that," she said.

"Thanks," John said.

"Are you heading back home?"

"Yeah, as soon as I can get up off this bench. It seems I could sit here forever. A cup of coffee and the heat of the sun. I believe that I'm beginning to forget that I'm a rancher. This city that seems alive. A curious place when you get use to it."

"They found the shooter, you know. He shot himself. He's dead."

"God. That little monkey-boy. It never seems to end."

"I know."

"It looks so ordered out there on the streets. Red light. Green light. One way. Right turn only. Cross here. Cross there."

"What you see here is just the surface. The face of the city. Look in the shadows. The cracks. There's life there too. It might not be pretty. But it's somebody's life."

"Don't you think that's worth writing about?"

"Ugliness is fear. People can only take so much of it."

"Tell the stories. Someone has to account for their lives. A record.

I don't know."

"It's safer in travel writing."

"Harley Buck told me once, the only journey worth traveling is from the head to the heart."

Alexandra Grove smiled then rose from the bench to leave. "Drive carefully, John Trickett," she said.

"I will," John said.

She leaned forward and kissed his cheek. It surprised him but he didn't mind the gesture. It somehow helped close the circle. His time in Toronto had come to an end. He watched her as she walked away, down University Avenue, and after a time she just melted into the city. Touched his cheek and finished his coffee. Thought it tasted just fine. Becoming partial.

chapter
TWENTY ONE

John Trickett would never be the same. His mind stretched now could never return to the way it was. That limited model of occupation, the days of Windrush that merged one into the other. The rut of endless routine. He was returning to that life with an emerging sense of reclamation. The hard-boiled work of a seeker that found more than a brother. Suffering and man's search for meaning. And the book on the front seat beside him as he retraced the contours of the Canadian Shield. Toronto still a mystery to him. Behind him now but present. As if he could never leave it. A haunting quality that evoked an endless chain of questions. Scenarios spinning.

He slowed as he passed through English River. Sonny Merlot slouched at the gas pumps and John sounded his horn. Sonny looked up and made no immediate sign of recognition, but as John looked in his side-mirror he saw Sonny's hand slowly come up. Stopped at his waist, then shot up over his head, waving as he ran out to the edge of the highway. It made John feel good. A connection with the inconceivable. A friend in English River.

The highway home was not so strange. John knew what would be around the next corner. No surprises. And the Tim Hortons in Kenora offered its comforts, that hot soothing elixir that made highway driving agreeable. He thought he might see that same girl in the drive-thru. She wasn't there and he didn't inquire. Likely she was with her grandmother in Swift Current as she said she would be. He drove the sun down for two days and on the third day hit the prairie flat out and never stopped until he came to Prosper. Through the desolate street with the old-timers still gawking at him from the sidewalk as if they had been there all the time. Looking as if he was just an apparition, something from some other world, or perhaps they were apparitions themselves, ghosts of the dirty thirties refusing to quit the prairie.

He pulled over into Patty's Cafe. It was boarded up. A cardboard for sale sign was tacked unenthusiastically to the door. Letters scratched over the word Nashville. He thought of Brock Kendall and wondered how he was making out with his songs. He hoped that he would be successful, his dream come true. Sand piled at the door step. Dried thistle scratching. It seemed that it had been closed for years. Had he been there at all? And the wind moaned and he remembered old Rose slumping to the floor as her daughter lay near death at her feet. Her old mind had forsaken her and Patty's life ended in tragedy. What of her now? He had no inkling to get out of the truck and look around. There was nothing there for him save for the lament of the wind that seemed keen for his attention.

John stopped in Swift Current and there in a nursing home he found his mother sitting by a window in a wheelchair. A row of elderly residents set before the sun like potted geraniums. Her eyes closed and her face raised to the heavens. A queer smile. Crooked. He knelt down and spoke to her. Softly. But her eyes never opened. Told her about Luke, but still she remained frozen. He wondered if she understood. He stayed with her for a time sharing whatever the moments could realize. Something he hoped. The closing circle of life. And as he left her in the flood of the sun he thought he saw the girl from Kenora sitting with her grandmother. He passed her and smiled but she seemed not to recognize him. He stopped to turn back but he felt too sad for conversation and checked himself and continued on his way.

He crossed the reception area on his way out the door and noticed on a table a copy of a newspaper, sections fanned like cards. And there it was, the life of Steven Sullivan. He sat on a sofa set there for visitors and residents and read Alex Grove's article. Read it over and over until he was filled with Steven's life and thought himself privileged somehow. A proper story of a short life that he knew would be of comfort to Mr. Sullivan. He silently thanked Alexandra Grove and put the paper down and sat there in his sadness and endings. There all around him. Sat there depleted until his energy returned.

Out across the southern plains he drove, through the Great Sand Hills and at last Maple Creek, a town in slow motion. Idling. No one in a particular hurry. John drove through it in less than a minute. A few cowboys turned to him as he passed. Waved with a flick of their fingers as if in response to an auctioneer's bidding. And then he could see the bump of the Cypress Hills in the distance and there before him, Windrush. He stopped along the highway and gawped at the lemon-yellow fields hurling against the blue arc of the sky. Those cabbage whites. Such sights he had seen before. But now his mind was empty of thoughts as he admired the rich textures of colour. A momentary gap in the mind-stream when thinking ceases and there remains something pure and undefinable. Beyond interpretation. But thoughts soon came rushing in as he pulled off the highway and turned up the long drive and stopped near the barn. Harley's dog Nug loafing in the shade. Nora out on the porch and Del and Mitch nowhere to be seen.

He eased out of the truck, his back stiff and sore and his stomach that had been cramping most of that day was causing some discomfort. Facing Nora was like that first glimpse of Toronto. They both had shadowed worlds better left to casual re-acquaintance lest one had the forbearance to withstand the plunge. He stretched his legs and placed his hand in the small of his back and arched and shrugged and rotated his head and flexed his knees. He noticed at once that

Windrush had a different feel about it. Something fresh. Familiar but strangely altered. As if it had been rearranged. The barns newly painted. The sky brightly blue. The contrast salient and undiluted. And as he stepped up to the porch something hadn't changed. The hot dry air and discord.

"John," Nora said. A tentative smile. "You decided to come home."

She stood with her arms folded, waiting for John to come to her. Fling his contrition upon her. The return of the foolhardy. But he just looked down at his feet. Couldn't look at her disapproval. Her indictment.

"Never said I wasn't." he said. Nug sauntered up onto the porch and leaned against his leg. Dogs were without such grievances. Greet a man happily under any circumstance.

Nora touched his arm as he passed through the front door.

"Where's Del and Mitch?" John said.

"Walter's gone, John," Nora said from the porch. She followed him into the house.

"What?" He met her in the hallway.

"Last night, in his sleep. I had no way of contacting you. If you had called…"

John shook his head. "Where are the boys?"

"They left."

"Left?"

"They had an opportunity to move into their dorm early and they took it. There was nothing holding them here."

"But, the ranch."

"They just followed your example, John. I made arrangements with Charlie Triphammer's boy to take off the canola."

"What about Harley? Why is his dog here?"

"We had words. I don't think you'll see Harley come back."

"I told him to keep things simple. That old fool. What happened?"

"Well, I told him to fuck off and he did."

"What did he do to deserve that, Nora?"

"You know, John, he was looking at me all concerned that day he came storming in here. He could see how upset I was over what happened in Toronto. He was about to say something. Like he knew it all. His point of view. I gave him a look, John, but he went ahead anyway. He said, 'Nora, don't take this personal, but sometimes a woman thinks she knows what's best for a man. Tries to tell him how to live his life. A man needs his space to think on things. A man carries a great load and no man more than John.'

"And I looked at him straight faced, his head bobbing fatherly like and his eyes a twinkle, and said, 'fuck off, Harley.' He left his silly old pride and his lazy dog."

John raked his hair with his fingers. A great gust of air. He rubbed his eyes as if that might clear his view of the matter, but it didn't change a thing and he staggered into the living room and collapsed onto the couch. "Fuck me," he said. "Fuck. Fuck. Fuck!"

Things were looking poorly in the Trickett house. His new perspective sullied. He felt no warm reunion with his wife. In fact he couldn't reconcile how he could love Nora in the long grass and despise her on the porch. She seemed to possess the quality of several different women. A woman to fit his every need. Except the one he needed the most, a wife to support Luke's homecoming.

Nora sat down beside him. Watching him. Her mouth open. Stunned it seemed by his use of language. "Where do we go from here, John?" she said.

John's head slumped forward. His chin on his chest. "Better go see my dad. I can't deal with anything else right now."

"Yeah," Nora said.

They drove to the hospital in Maple Creek and not a word between them. Throats clogged with their differences. John knew Nora blamed him for Del and Mitch's early departure from Windrush. He couldn't fault them for leaving. The way he left things. Besides there was a whole other world out there. He knew that much now. And Nora hadn't asked about Luke and the question hung like something malevolent between them, a thing wounded and in need of succor. John couldn't leave it unsaid for long as he had come to understand that wounds left alone would fester until the pain was unbearable. But still he was paralyzed by his conditioning, his role, what he had to lose. The complexities of his marriage that had surfaced. Pushed and pulled by his atonement.

A nurse lead them down a flight of stairs. Then down a long hallway lit with a bare light bulb to a door that read Morgue. It was a cold and desolate place. She told them to wait outside but the door was ajar and John watched her open a curtain and pull out a stainless steel drawer. His father on a chrome platter wheeled out for closure. Words he could not hear. Then she let them in and left them alone. A plastic smile. In the room it was colder still and John moved to his father's side. Nora followed him and peered over his shoulder. She looked down at Walter Trickett and gasped then backed away. She wasn't prepared for his appearance. She hurried out of the room with her hands to her mouth.

It didn't seem like John's father at all. All likeness gone. His mouth jacked open in a muted bawl and a thin sheet draped over him. Hard ridges of bone and a smell of death. John had no sense of his father in that old yellow hide. The utter stillness of his dead body. He touched his cheek and it was cadaverously chilled. He could only look up to the ceiling, to a divine hand that might be there, but there was nothing but water stains and the faith that raised his head to that inviolable space.

"I found Luke and he's coming home, Dad," he began. "Not right away. But soon. I'm sorry I left when I did, but I just had to find him. It seemed I had no choice in the matter. I don't think you'll blame me for it. You know how much Mom suffered. I promised her. He's coming home to Windrush, Dad. The two of us like we planned."

His voice was cracking badly and he could no longer speak. He turned away and Nora standing outside the door with her eyes closed and tears streaming down onto her blouse. John placed his hand on her shoulder to console her, but she shook her head and made a feral scream and ran down the hallway.

chapter
TWENTY TWO

Walter Trickett left instructions. What photograph to display in his honour. A floral arrangement of tiger lilies, red and white carnations and hyacinth. No organ music and no tears. Cremation and no church service. Instead he asked that a memorial be held at Windrush and Harley Buck read the eulogy. The former was doable but the latter was a great assumption. Still the obituary was posted in the Maple Creek newspaper and that Saturday in the middle of August arrived dusty and hot and hell on ranchers. In the ranch house kitchen Nora and Gerty Buck made tea and sandwiches cut in quarters, butter tarts and date bars while Harley stood outside his truck in the driveway having fits. Flakes of dead skin freckled the shoulders on his dark suit jacket. John shaking his head sympathetically.

"It's a cruel thing to do to a friend, John." Tucked a chaw behind his lip like the Godfather.

"I guess my dad thought it might be an honour. You two go a longs ways back, Harley."

"She told me to fuck off, John. Excuse my language, but did you know that? Don't care to tattle on anyone, especially your wife. But how in God's name do you think I can stand up before her and speak about Walter? No one ever spoke to me like that before, John. It's a troublesome thing for a man."

"You'll be speaking to everyone, Harley."

"Don't you believe it. She'll be all over me if I slip up. She troubles me, John. I mean no disrespect. But she troubles me. The one person on earth."

"I know, Harley." John stroked his chin to assuage his bewilderment. Harley Buck whipped by blond accountant.

"Damn, John, I don't mean to sound ungrateful."

"I know. If it makes it easier don't look at her. Look at the wall or something."

"I'd prefer to get drunk."

"I don't think you have time, Harley. And I wouldn't have recommended it if you had mentioned it earlier. You wouldn't want to be further disadvantaged."

"No, I suppose not, but I wouldn't remember anything which would likely be a good thing."

"I thought of that myself on occasion."

"Hell, John, Tricketts aren't drinkers. Walter liked his whiskey now and then. I know that much. But mostly you all like to be sober when you suffer."

"What does that mean?"

"Nothing. Just my nerves. Nothing at all."

As they stood there, mourners came by in ones and twos and offered John their condolences. Cupped his hands. Dressed in their best suits. Dresses meant for church. Floral prints from the Sears summer catalogue.

"Well, did you write something, Harley?"

"Yeah, I scribbled down a few things. Speaking about someone's life in just a few minutes is not an easy thing to do."

"He'll appreciate it, Harley. And I appreciate it. And my family."

"I haven't seen your boys, John." Looked around. Down the row of cars and trucks lining the driveway. He had to squint against the glare of the sun on the windshields. Heat waves pooling on the gravel. A column of poplars still as death and swallows idle on the telephone wires. Clouds on the eastern and western horizons like book ends. Harley reading the landscape like scripture.

"It seems they won't be able to attend." Nothing more. He hadn't seen them for awhile. He knew they were going to leave. Strike out on their own. But he suddenly felt empty, lost. He needed to see them. Something that needed to be said.

"I'm sorry." Leaned over and spat to avoid spoiling his suit.

"Yeah. University, you know. It'll keep them busy. But Albert Triphammer will help us out with the harvest. A hell of a good worker that Albert."

Harley nodded. A perplexed screwing of his eyes. Then he swung around to Nug loping up to him. Moaning something pitiful. Dancing around him, rubbing up on his leg like a cat. Tried to jump up but his front paws wouldn't leave the ground. Old age and gravity.

"Thought I abandoned you, did you, old dog?" he said. "I knew where you were." He reached down and scratched under his ears. Old Nug rolled his eyes. Orgasmic. "You know, John, you'll have to tell me all about Toronto. I still can't get my mind around what happened."

"I think about it a lot, Harley. It seems like someone else's story. Not mine."

"Yeah, well you've been through enough to last a while, friend. Didn't happen to see Johnny Bower, did you?"

Then Nora on the porch. "It's time, John."

"Better lose that plug, Harley. I don't want to see you choke on it."

In the house a crowd in the kitchen that spilled out into the dining room and living room. The pervasive fragrance of hyacinth. Old pictures out for reflection and recollection. That favorite photograph of Walter Trickett with a coyote slung over a wire fence that made the women grieve for the coyote. Sandwiches on napkins held waist high. The raising of tea cups and muted conversation. Rare chuckles.

Restrained. And John making his way through the mourners, shaking hands, kissing perfumed cheeks dusted with rouge. "He was a good man," from their lips. Not a word about the gossip. A marriage in trouble and picking sides.

John clinked his tea cup as it was time to introduce Harley. Thanked everyone for coming and looked around the living room but couldn't find him. He began to worry that he bolted, succumbed to the pressure. Then he called out for him and all heads turned and after a momentary delay Harley made his appearance. Paced in the hallway. He made his way through the crowd and stood beside John. All red about his cheeks. Flushed and sweat beads clustered above his upper lip. His scalp raw from feverish raking. Pink through the snowy bristles. There were chairs along the wall and the mourners sat down and those without chairs stood to listen. He cleared his throat and took a drink of water from a glass John set out for him.

Nora and Gerty came out from the kitchen. Nora stood against the wall opposite to him. In his direct line of vision. Arms crossed. Intimidating. Her eyes heavy with acrimony. She was dressed smartly in a navy blue suit. Humbled every woman in the house. Gerty went to Harley and swatted the flakes from his shoulders. He didn't seem to notice.

He removed a sheet of paper and his reading glasses from his suit pocket and began his eulogy by recalling life on the prairie when he and Walter Trickett were young men. Stories of the great depression. Dust and grasshoppers and neighbours who had to count on one another. The war and friends they lost. A cowboy's hard life and now the uncertain future. A way of life in doubt. Things to be grateful for. He stammered and took his water and glanced up now and then but did not look towards Nora. Pulled his collar away from his neck with his thick index finger. A stream of perspiration down his temples. Then he put away his sheet of paper and stood silently for a moment. His head down. He seemed to be stuck. Then he took out a handkerchief and wiped his face and forehead. Ran it over his suffering scalp.

"You alright?" John whispered leaning towards him.

"Yeah."

"Are you done?"

"Not quite," he said. He raised his head, removed his glasses and looked right at Nora Trickett. His eyes now certain and unwavering as cross-hairs. "I just want to finish," he continued, "by saying Walter Trickett raised two boys. Johnny and Luke. John here, you all know. And Luke, well you all heard the news. John found him. He's in the hospital in Regina. He's very sick, but under that sickness there's a real person. We can't forget that. His illness is not his fault. And he's coming home to Windrush. Yes, and there's no better day to tell you this. It is the highest regard I can give to Walter Trickett. I would ask that you all bow your heads for a moment and pray for Luke. Pray for his recovery. Soon John and Luke and Windrush will be back together. Luke's rightful place in the world. Their dream. The way it was meant to be. A miracle I would say." He nodded to reaffirm his assertion. "Thank you," he concluded.

He dropped his eyes from Nora who glared back menacing. Outraged. Betrayed in her own house. He knew what he had done. The evangelical resonance. He left her there with the sympathizers, tearful and inspired, turned Maple Creek against her and hastened for the back door.

It was some stunt. Harley Buck's moment of retribution. It didn't matter to John whether Harley was right or wrong, he knew he had to move fast to catch up to him as Nora was already out the door with murder on her mind. But she caught him before he could get to his truck. Called him like a gunslinger.

"Harley Buck, you bastard!" she shrilled. "You chickenshit bastard!"

Harley turned to her and threw his hands up in surrender. "I just want to leave," he said. "I'm not going to fight with you, Nora. I'm done."

John stepped up between them. "I think you two better have a time out," he said. The mourners came out onto the porch. Mouths open before a spectacle. Like cattle considering things unknown to them.

"I'm not done here," Nora said leaning forward into Harley's face. Her hands raised at her sides as if she was about to draw on him. A pistol on each hip.

"Alright," John said, "then you better deal with whatever's going on between you once and for all. Right here." He stepped back like a referee at a main event.

Nora went right at him. A rapid pummeling. "How dare you fling that in my face. In my own home. You're a fucking coward, Harley. A used-up old coward!"

"No, I'm no coward, Nora. I may be afraid of you. A fact that distresses me some. But I'm not a coward."

"You think you know what's best for John."

"I know that you blame him for Del and Mitch leaving."

"What would you know about that? You never had children. You haven't earned the right to talk about my children, asshole!"

"It is true. Gerty and I weren't blessed with children. I suppose that's why I can see things you can't. Windrush is sick. Something that's never been dealt with."

"What the hell do you mean, Harley?"

"I'm talking about Luke, damn it. You denied his existence for years. You helped John get through some tough times and we're all grateful for it. For a while there I thought we were going lose them both. You helped him get over Luke. But he didn't die, Nora. It's my opinion that Del and Mitch had no choice in the matter. They could no longer sit by and watch what it was doing to their family. A painful thing to witness."

"You silly old man. You have no idea what you're talking about. You've never had sons. That chilling fear that they'd turn sick. Like him. Everyday I live it, Harley."

"Fear doesn't change a thing, Nora," Harley said. In the eye of the storm he found a still point. A place where fear could no longer touch him. He was calm and soft spoken, aligned with his prairie wisdom. "Our minds don't know any better. Fear is our resistence to what's in front of us. We have no control what will happen, but we sure as hell can control how we respond to it. We can either kick and scream or accept it. John's Uncle Tommy had the sickness and hung himself as a young man. But they never had proper treatments back then. There's help now days. You can't just beat it with a stick and hope it won't happen. I'm a bit surprised a liberated woman such as you wouldn't know that."

Nora's face went ashen. The fight seeped out of her. "Tommy?" she said. "Did you know about that, John?" A quarter turn with her eyes slanting downward. Couldn't look at him.

"Yeah, I knew about it." Head down.

The mourners began to shuffle past them to their cars and trucks. Pats on their shoulders. Eyes averted. The women of Maple Creek didn't know what to make of Nora Trickett. Thought it might be her liberal west coast upbringing. Soon there was just the three of them. Gerty on the porch cleaning up. She never heard a thing.

"That's about all I can handle for one day," Harley said. He opened the door to his truck and Nug sauntered out of the shade and he lifted him up onto the seat and slid in behind him. Sounded the horn for Gerty. Through the open window. "It seems to me, John, that you should've had that conversation with your wife. Not this silly old cowboy. And would you mind going over and getting that old woman."

The next day the blanched prairie simmered beneath a mule sun and John and Nora backed into their corners. Stayed away from each other until dinner. The safe limits of estrangement where nothing was gained except temporary relief and the distance between them drifting like pack ice. The awkwardness of strangers at the dinner table. Words caught in their throats, unwilling to venture out into the world. Agoraphobic. The tension between them ran thick as winter oil.

Then Nora's eyes squeezed to desperation. She poured a glass of wine and set the half-empty bottle on the table and leaned forward on her elbows. A capricious grin. "Since you've forgotten how to speak, John Trickett," she said, "I'll tell you something."

John looked up from his dinner. Had to look at her now. Waited for it and felt the pull of muscles that cradled his abdomen. Wondered where his new found confidence went to. Hoped it was something about the weather. The impact of weevils. The expansion of seed oil or another load of cattle to the Cowtown Livestock Exchange.

"I've been thinking about Harley," she said, "standing there spinning that Will Rogers crap of his. Did you hear him, John?"

"I had to pry you two apart," John said on the cusp of levity to appease himself. "I didn't know he was going to say all that. But most times Harley is right about things."

"Then you believe what he told you was right?"

"What are you getting at, Nora?" John said flippantly. He knew she was just beginning. In fact he sensed that he wouldn't be able to stop her once she started on him. He was thinking that he preferred the silence to one of her tirades. His silence perturbed her more than anything. It was a form of resistance, recreant violence, behaviour contrary to his predictability that he exorcized in the ravines of Toronto.

"I know you think I'm a bitch, John. I just know it."

"Come on, Nora. That's not true." Shakes his head but was beginning to think it.

"Damn it, John,"

"Don't, Nora."

"You resent me because I don't want Luke to come back to Windrush. It sounds cold, doesn't it? Yes, I'm a bloody bitch. I'll say it right here. And look at you. Shut up like a fucking clam. Why won't you talk to me? You never heard a word Harley said. Not a fucking word, John Trickett!"

John stared down at his mashed potatoes. Picked with his fork. How could he respond to that? Talking like Steven Sullivan. He could only feel the hard jolt of it.

"Say something!"

"You've been drinking."

"Tell me what part of what I just said isn't true."

John pushed himself away from the table. Struggled to stay. Fought to face her, to stand up to the fire within her that sizzled like bacon. Like Harley. But he couldn't defend himself, rebuke the telling slices. He left her there with the memory of his limitations.

chapter
TWENTY THREE

Summer waned. A lonely affair. The air still and breathless and the smell of agronomic disaster. The pall of drought cast upon the land like a plague that made life a suffering feast to pessimists and all out strain to optimists. The canola flowers shed their yellow blossoms and the green pods formed and soon browned enough for harvest. Albert Triphammer worked the cool evenings on the swather until all the plants were cut and laid upon the stubble. Albert was a farm boy who had no further ambitions in life than to sit atop a John Deere. The great green machine. And ten days later Albert picked up the swath with the combine and the seed was separated and trucked to an elevator in town.

John took advantage of Albert's assistance at Windrush and visited Luke. Day trips at first, just to sit with him in his room. Luke wasn't ready to visit his mother, that promise fulfilled, the happy ending that was more a dream than a possibility. John read all he could find on Luke's illness. Stuffed a Schizophrenia Society of Saskatchewan booklet in his back pocket like a pair of gloves. Talked to him without a response and never stopped because of it. He developed a relationship with the nurses, called them by name and expressed his gratitude. He wanted the best of care for Luke and they appreciated his dedication. Said they read about him in the paper. Then Luke was well enough to leave the hospital to walk the grounds for short periods. Slack-boned and nervous and unable to answer John's questions about his day. Simple things that could only elicit an occasional troubled glance. And rides in John's truck to Pilot Butte and Balgonie and one day to Indian Head. Luke with his face pressed against the window with the prairie speeding by. Ducks in ponds that would rise and settle in great autumn flocks. And John watched him there on the Trans-Canada highway, observed his movements, expressions, responses. Imagined the Luke he used to know and wondered how he could possibly be the same person. What was the meaning beneath his unremembered life? Thought of the book on his night stand.

And on the day before Luke was discharged from the hospital, John attended a family support group meeting and the facilitator gave him a discharge planning checklist: medicine information and dosage instructions, living arrangements with a group home in Regina, community care referrals, dentists and eye care, precautions on suicide, smoking and behaviour variables and expectations; the need to speak slow and use a low tone, avoid confusion, explain, the need for structure, offer praise, avoid over stimulation and criticism, mastery of self-care, don't be too inquisitive, how to overcome difficult communication and enjoy his company in other ways; televison, music, memories of childhood, reading, be forgetful for his benefit to encourage participation and responsibility. Be a friend, help him belong.

And when Thanksgiving arrived, John Trickett knew that the time had come. Del and Mitch were returning for the holiday. He invited Harley and Gerty to dinner and was surprised and pleased that Harley accepted and Nora never said a word of objection. And then he finally dropped that other shoe. He was bringing Luke home for the first time in twenty five years. A week to reunite with Windrush. Nephews he never knew. And Nora.

He left early to pick up Luke from the group home. Clear and cold. Frosted brush along the fence lines and the glitter of field stubble coppering down the long lanes of the sun. The proclamation of high-up geese and shifting clouds of blackbirds and swallows leaving, hurrying southward. He gave them just passing notice. He was worried about how he felt about Luke. Not his memories, but his detached feelings that hadn't changed since that first glimpse of him in the shadows of the Don River Valley. It distressed him and he didn't know why. He wanted to tell Nora about it, but he couldn't. Stuck like a mired bull. Grieving for his parents and his marriage, a sadness filling his hallow inner-world that deepened the day Steven Sullivan was murdered and hadn't let up. The cast of characters in his journey that seemed held together by some common theme. Something about them. Something within him unrecognized.

And there he was in Swift Current bringing Luke home as he promised, to his mother slipping from the world into a world impenetrable and bleak. John tried to tell Luke about her, that she was waiting for him. So happy she was to have found him at last. A son taken from her. But he showed no measure of a response, nothing but that restless confusion. News of their father drew no reaction as well. Perhaps he had abandoned them, scuttled his memories in order to survive.

And as he pulled into the care facility he drew a long breath. What will he do? What will she do? A reunion so poignant and astounding that the mere thought of it made him feel hopeful, too hopeful perhaps, that indeed all that he had been through was worth the tenderest of moments. He took Luke by the arm and met an attendant who guided them to her room. She was in her room sitting in a chair staring at a small screen television. It was turned off.

"Mom, I have someone here to see you," John said. A prayer to himself.

He helped Luke to her bed and he sat beside her, their knees touching, so close they were now. So distant. This is it, John thought, the subtle touching of mother and son. No words or recognition, eyes wandering, fixated, empty. Detached. There was nothing to do, to force, to concoct or insist. It was just that. He allowed them to sit in their in silence, in their world. Perhaps it was there where all reckoning was at work, souls engaged in reconciliation, beyond the suffering acquaintance of flesh. The moment remained as long as it could. And Windrush called from this world and John kissed his mother on the cheek and gathered Luke and left.

The welcoming committee out on the front porch. Harley and Gerty with their arms wide open. Big grins. Del and Mitch withdrawn, shy, hands in their pockets and Nora behind the screen door like a phantom. As if she was already half gone. They would have seen the truck pull off the highway and come up the long drive. Poplar leaves kicking up behind. Scattering then settling. And they would have seen the two figures, John behind the wheel wearing that high-crowned hat and the other figure slouched against the window.

John got out of the truck and glanced up to the porch and nodded. Affirmed the reception. He went over to Luke's side of the truck and opened the door. "We're home, Luke," he said. "Windrush." He spoke gently and the sound of it surreal like the words in his many dreams.

Luke stared blankly at him. Then over to the barns and up at the sky. His eyes brightened, capturing the blue dome of the world. They moved slowly, steadily. Evaluating. But he didn't move. Held to the seat by his seatbelt.

"Do you need a hand there , John?" Harley called out.

John stepped back and pushed the brim of his hat up with his thumb. "I think we're okay, Harley," he said.

"Harley Buck," Luke said softly.

It startled John. Surprised him. Delighted him. "That's right, Luke. Harley Buck. Lives right across the highway." Pointed and Luke looked over his shoulder. Unbuckled his seatbelt.

Luke swung his legs around and stepped onto the firm ground of Windrush. Stepping on glass, tentative. He was slight, thinner than he ever was. It seemed to John that the group home dressed him like an old man on a summer outing. Light coloured slacks and white shirt. Beige golf-jacket. Walking shoes with velcro fasteners. Looking for the front nine. His black hair was cut short, sheared at the temples where it bristled silver. A slight stoop and his hands at his sides like accessories. Indifferent to the cold.

John removed his belongings. A change of clothes in a plastic bag. A carton of cigarettes. "Come on, Luke," he said taking him by the arm, "you're about to meet your family." Luke shuffled behind him and stopped at the bottom of the stairs that led to the porch. Looked past everyone watching him, his eyes surveying the white house that had not changed at all. Not even the old wooden chairs and the scuffed paint from the drag of tired feet or the screen door that snapped shut to keep out the summer flies. He was remembering. So it seemed to John and the others who did not speak, but stood motionless, silent as if in anxious anticipation of an infant's first step. Witness to a miracle manifesting there before them. The healing moment. Eyes misted and faces bright and awed. Bursting. Their holding breaths. Waiting for the sweet words of intellect and reason to sing from his lips. The song of restoration.

John stood there on the porch and waited for that moment that seemed plausible and imminent, a rudimentary expectation. But Luke was unable to move or speak, immobilized it seemed, by the reckoning of things lost to him. And all at once a certain doubt pervaded the confines of the porch like an audience caught in the silent terror of an actor who has forgotten his lines. John quickly seized the scene and stepped down to Luke and took him by the arm and turned to his family with a reassuring smile.

"It's freezing out here," he said, "let's go inside."

Luke crept into the house languid and cautious and needed to be guided into the living room. Sat down on a corner recliner. The others sat too, but John remained standing and reintroduced Luke to the Bucks who he still remembered. He stared at them which seemed a recognition of sorts. Enough for Gerty to remind him how cute he was as a little boy.

"Those blue eyes," she said, "like delphinium. As blue as can be. The most beautiful eyes that I had ever seen."

"Hogwash," Harley said, throwing his hands up. "I thought I had the most beautiful eyes you'd ever seen. Like Paul Newman, you told me." Laughed and snorted and slapped his knee.

"You're so full of yourself, Harley Buck," Gerty said. Blushed and turned away.

Luke watched them both. His eyes from one to the other. Watched Harley's arm swing up and down. The slap. And John always watching him.

"And this is my oldest son, Del," John said. Placed his hand on his shoulder.

Del stepped up to Luke and offered his hand. "Uncle Luke," he said. An affable grin.

Luke's hand came up slow and heavy and Del took it in his and shook it, but Luke's hand never closed and folded and Del let it go and stepped back, disconcerted. Wiped his hand discreetly on the side of his leg. Some involuntary aversion.

"And my youngest Mitch," John said.

Mitch did the same thing as his brother but this time Luke's hand never came up. Something startled him.

"What are you doing here?" Luke said slowly. A subtle rocking.

Mitch didn't know quite what to do and turned to his father and shrugged.

"Luke, that's Mitch, your nephew. You've never met him before. He's here for Thanksgiving dinner and to meet you." Knelt down to him. "I know this a lot for you. But just relax. Alright, Luke? Everything is okay now."

Luke nodded. A side glance to Mitch. To the others.

And John turned to Nora standing in the hallway. That troubled look of hers. What Luke said to Mitch, he knew. "Nora," he said, "you remember Luke."

Of course she did. Fool thing to say. He had defied her but she remained, never threatening to leave him if he brought Luke home. Now he was home and she was preparing dinner for him. Soon to sit down and give thanks. But that remark to Mitch was buzzing around the inside of her head like a hornet and John could hear the muted drone of it in his own head.

Nora came out wearing her apron and stood at the entrance to the living room. Fiddling with the apron strings. The threshold she didn't wish to cross. "Yes," she said. A smile that pained her.

"Luke, my wife Nora," John said. "Do you remember?"

Luke's head tilted to look past him. Cocked like a parrot. "Nora," he said plainly. An inflection pleased and ardent. How good to see you.

That seemed to still the rattle and hum and Nora returned to the kitchen and Gerty followed her and conversation started among the men, talk of hockey and football, talk that skirted the plight of the prairie economy and did not let up until Nora called them to dinner. The rising and passing of words and all was quiet save for the tic of the clock on the mantle and the sound of Luke in the corner rocking. And eyes that measured the pendulum's swing.

chapter
TWENTY FOUR

John took Luke upstairs to a spare room and helped him put away his things. A plain room with a bed and night table and a chest of drawers, a curtained window that looked out over the eastern rangeland. Kept the room simple and uncluttered. Single painting on one wall, a watercolour of a wildflower. Purple aster with a skipper butterfly balanced on a petal. Luke sat on the bed and admired the painting as John pointed to the bathroom so he could wash up before dinner. Asked him if he could come down the stairs on his own and he nodded that he could. Gave Luke that responsibility.

The great Trickett table was set and everyone seated save for Luke who hadn't made his appearance, the turkey carved and trimmed and side dishes steaming and mouths slavering. Brussel sprouts and yams, turnips and apple. Mashed potatoes and breaded stuffing with bacon and peppered with aromatic sage. Pickles and sliced beets and olives. Hot rolls and chilled cranberries. Pumpkin pies on the side table. Saskatoon berry tarts golden crusted. They were all eager to indulge in the offerings that Nora prepared, the likes of which John had never seen at Windrush, not even from his own mother. A special occasion it was, and the fact of the matter, the care and attention that Nora put into it, so impressed John that for a moment he thought himself guilty of some unmistakable crime against her and had a notion to ask for her forgiveness.

But the motive behind such effort was not so clear to John. Some settlement with Harley? A celebration for Del and Mitch, her boys home again? An offering to Luke, his memory, his return, acceptance at long last? He watched her as Luke came down the stairs and into the dining room and took his seat beside him, his eyes finding her each time she looked away. She was not overjoyed it seemed to him. Something unreal about her civility. Some pretense there. But still a family together and Luke among them.

John poured a half measure of wine into Luke's glass and made a toast to Windrush and everyone raised their glasses and murmured some sentiment and Harley said, "here, here," and Nora smiled thinly and all seemed well enough. There was something about good food, the bounty of heaping platters and wine to unhinge rusty tongues when all could be forgotten and forgiven, as if grace arose from the comfort of friends and family to appease the miseries of formidable days.

Harley was curious about the boys. "So tell me, Del," he said, "what are you and Mitch up to at the University of Alberta?"

"Do you mean school or girls, Mr. Buck?" Del answered cheekily.

"What the hell do I know about school?" Harley chortled.

A chorus of laughter erupted and all was gay and warm and Luke more puzzled than giddy, his head down shyly. And Nora too, saw the humour in Harley's wit and forgot herself for an instant, but swiftly raised her fingers to her lips as if to censure the pleasure of laughter.

"Seriously," Harley said duly pleased. Put down his fork to paw. "What is it you boys are studying up there in Edmonton?"

"They call it the School of Mining and Petroleum Engineering," Del said.

"I know that much, Del," Harley said, "but what they heck are you learning?"

Del winked at Mitch. "Balanced drilling," he said.

"Thermal recovery," Mitch said.

"Heavy oil and cold sand production technology." Del's turn. Both all grins.

"Fluid flow through porous media."

"Steam assisted gravity drainage and its variations."

"Interface coupling phenomena." Back and forth like a swede saw.

Harley's hand came up. "Alright you smart-asses, I hope you come up with something other than oil up there. Piston engines and that little buggy on Mars. What the hell is that all about?"

"We'll have oil for a while yet, Mr. Buck," Mitch said. "The world economy depends on it."

"There must be something else."

"Syngas and ethanol," Mitch said.

"There's hydrogen," Del added. "Non-carbon fuel, green-house gas neutral."

"Cow shit if you can find enough cattle left out here on the prairie," Mitch concluded.

"You won't have to look farther than this here table," Harley cackled.

Nora looked on at her two sons and beamed proudly. A match for Harley. Took great delight in the revelry in her house. A mother's dream. But John was distracted by Luke. Watched the movement of his shoulder. His slouch and his glare at Mitch. Then Luke turned to Del, leaned forward in his chair and spoke under his breath. Teeth clenched and the muscles in his neck like flying buttresses. Then louder and all mirth vanished, whisked away by an unsettling wind.

"Get him away from my house, Billy," he said.

That look of sheer quandary around the table. A sentence without relevance and meaning so it seemed. But John feared what it might be. Echoes of the haunting Don River.

"Luke, what is it?" he said.

Luke lowered his head as if too heavy to bear under the silent scrutiny of averting eyes and lifted his shirt and exposed the bullet wound on his belly. A star incision, pink welded. Like a crucifix branded into his flesh. "You did that," he said to Mitch angrily.

Things were falling apart and John pushed away from the table and took Luke by the arm. "Come, Luke," he said, "I'll take you up to your room so you can rest." He tried to smile, force some reason upon the scene.

"Who is Billy?" Mitch said noticeably upset. Turned to his mother and shrugged.

John led Luke out of the dining room."You reminded him of someone, Mitch," he said over his shoulder. "Not to worry. He's just tired, that's all."

Dinner continued without John or Luke. A polite affair that could not sustain any measure of revelry. A sobering pall. And dessert was served and tea poured and then talk ran out and Harley and Gerty stood out on the porch and said their goodbyes. John came down and apologized. Harley pawed and looked up at the starless roof of the world.

"Snow tomorrow," he said. "Cold as hell the day after."

The boys watched television and Nora cleaned up in the kitchen. Luke was asleep and John laid in bed thumbing through *Man's Search for Meaning* looking for clues. A glimpse of Steven Sullivan's bloodied body. 'That fucking homo, eh, Zeke.' Put the book down and stared up at the ceiling and listened to Nora. Wondered what she was thinking while she scraped the stack of plates. Rinsed pots and soaked the turkey roaster. The banging of cupboards to raise the dead. Then nothing coming from the kitchen and murmurs from the living room. Reassuring them. And when Nora came to bed John was still awake.

"The answers are not in there," she said. Whispering.

"I wish they were," John said.

"It's not what you thought it would be."

"No."

"He's very ill, John."

"Yeah."

"You thought he would come back to Windrush and everything would be alright."

"I hoped it would."

"That look he gave Mitch, that's what frightens me, John."

"I know."

"You think I've been a bitch."

"Why do you always say that?"

"It's just a good word. A scratching, clawing word. It's how I feel sometimes."

"What would you call me then?"

"A prick. Sometimes you can be a prick."

"I know it."

"And I know it's not his fault. He didn't ask for it. But I can't change what happened to him and you can't change what happened no matter how much guilt you feel. That's a fact. If you want answers, John, all you had to do was look at those two young men sitting at the table tonight. So proud. The way they looked at you. For your attention. Your approval. Your acceptance. That's where your attention is needed, John. You're a father first."

"I was a brother before I was a father."

"I know that."

"Luke just needs a chance and I'm all he's got." A sigh squeezed from the weight of the world. "Good God, Nora, I didn't choose him over the boys. It wasn't like that."

"I know." Consoling now.

"Ruined your dinner. Sorry."

"Well, we had our moments even if you weren't listening."

"It was Luke."

"Yeah, well." A nasal humph. "Who did he see in Mitch?"

"The kid who shot him."

"Great. What does that mean?"

"He was confused. There is a resemblance."

"John?"

"I know. Don't say it."

chapter
TWENTY FIVE

In the morning John Trickett rose and hobbled over to the window and tipped the blinds. Rubbed his eyes and scratched his backside. Private rituals. Light snow. He planned to give Luke a tour of the ranch. Help feed the remaining herd of Belgian Blues. Stack irrigation pipe if he was up to it. Fresh air and hard work made a man feel more alive. Drove out frustration. Seeped out of every pore.

Nora watched him in the achromatic light that hid flaws. Forgiving sleep. "What is it doing out there?" she said.

"Just like Harley said."

"The boys should leave before it sticks to the highway."

"Yeah."

"Come back to bed, John," Nora said. Threw the blankets aside.

John turned back to her. Backlit against the window. Hesitant as if there was something more.

"You might want to take Luke back before it gets too bad out here," Nora said casually. An inflection like sugar. She pulled her nightshirt up over her head. Her pale skin sprawling velvet across the bed. Nipples rising like frozen berries. Sweet.

John stood in the cold shadows. An invitation to love her. Her body. The simplicity of men coursing in hot blood, a genetic imperative. The tingling of his scrotum and the stiffening. The slow steady rise. It had been a while, the latent longing. Soon he would lose his mind. Then he turned back quickly to the window and looked out to the barn. A sudden taking back of his brain at the cusp of surrender. Something was missing.

"Truck's gone," he said with masked consternation.

"Gone? What do you mean gone?" Nora said.

"Tire tracks in the snow heading down the reservoir road."

"One of the boys out for a last look around. You know how Mitch loves the snow."

"Yeah, most likely," John said. He calmly pulled on his jeans and his shirt. Turned away to buckle up hastily. Left Nora sitting up in bed with the blankets covering her breasts like some Hollywood minx. Cowboy jilted.

"Let me know," she said curtly as John left the bedroom.

He made his way to Del and Mitch's room and knocked on the door and opened it. Del looked up sleepy and swollen-eyed. The firm glare of his father. Mitch's bed was empty.

"Where's your brother, Del?" he said.

"Downstairs, I expect," Del said. "You know him, up at the crack."

John nodded. "Didn't say anything about taking the truck out, did he?"

"No. What's going on, Dad?"

"Nothing," John said. "Truck's gone. He must have taken it for a drive to the reservoir. Not to worry. Go back to sleep."

He left Del to his slumber and closed the door behind him and stood in the hallway and stared at Luke's door. He was out of breath and his heart began to race and he hadn't even moved. He had to get it over with lest his heart explode. He rushed to the door and opened it and found that Luke was gone. Somehow he knew. No sign of him save for his pill bottle on the night table. The lid was missing and the vial was empty. It didn't make sense to John. If he had taken them all it would likely have killed him. Reproached himself for not keeping

Luke's medicine.

He left the bedroom and ran down the hall and as he passed the bathroom he noticed the light still on. He turned by habit and there on the floor beside the toilet, a single tablet. He picked it up and held it in the light. A rush of cold foreboding pouring down his neck.

Then Nora called from the bedroom. "What's going on, John?"

And his brain began to conjure up all manner of scenarios as he descended the stairs two at a time, and in the background of his frantic thoughts, he knew well enough not to answer her. He flew through the kitchen and out onto the back porch. Swept the washed out horizon. The angled flakes unhurried. Then without thinking he ran around to the front of the house in his stocking feet. Saw where the truck had been and the long arc of tread leading away. He followed footprints back to the front porch. Two sets. He wondered if they left together. Then Nora burst out of the front door. In her fist something burning. Eyes cutting like lasers.

"He's got the gun , John," she said. "I found this on the floor outside the closet." She held out her hand. A .22 long rifle shell. "The closet was open. It's gone, John. He's got the fucking gun!"

"Stop it, Nora, we don't know that. Mitch likely took it for target practice."

"Then where's Luke, with him?"

"I don't know."

"We better call the police."

"What? We don't know anything."

"You heard what he said to Mitch. He thinks he's someone else. My God, John, he could have taken Mitch at gunpoint. He could shoot him. Mitch could be killed. Can't you see?"

"Hold on, Nora. Just shut up!"

Del poked his head out the door. His father out in the snow in his socks. His mother spitting bolts of fury. "What happened?" he said.

"Come inside, John." Nora said. Tossed John the bullet. Shook her head all the way to the kitchen.

"We don't know, Del," John said. "Trucks gone and so are Mitch and Luke."

"The .22's missing."

"Which one has it?" Del said. A fearful question to his father.

John opened his hand. The single tablet and the .22 shell like lethal crumbs leading to annihilation. Let them fall through his fingers onto the floor. "He flushed his medication," he said gravely.

"Damn it, John, I'm calling the police. We can't take a chance!"

John stood there in the kitchen with his head cupped in his hands. He fell back against the counter struggling for a clear head, a sound course of action amidst the anxiety that threatened to fog his brain. Give in to Nora.

"John?"

"Alright," he said finally. "I'm going to call Harley. Get his truck. That rental car of yours won't do at all, Del. We can follow the tracks down the reservoir road and try to catch up to them. They could be at Grandpa Trickett's old hunting shack near the reservoir. Luke liked to go there with that .22. And don't call the police, Nora. Nothing good will come of it. If they think for a minute that Luke's holding Mitch, someone's going to get killed. I'm certain of it."

"You better be right about this, John. If anything happens to Mitch…"

"Luke will listen to me."

"Who knows what his state of mind will be?"

"I don't know. I just don't know."

John called Harley and soon he came pounding up the driveway fish-tailing in the snow and as he turned in front of the house he slammed on the brakes and skidded sideways and stopped. He reached across the seat and opened the passenger door. Nora looked on from the porch and Harley touched the brim of his felt stetson to acknowledge her. She held onto Del as if he might be snatched by the wind. A tormented gaze.

John jumped into the truck and Harley jammed the stick into low gear and the truck bucked and spun and swerved onto the track that lead to the reservoir road.

"Some worried," Harley said.

John turned back to her. Gusts of snow obscuring her mother-bear ferocity. Damned her intractable nature. "You talking about me or Nora, Harley?"

"Doesn't much matter, John. Sounds a bit dicey."

"Can you drive this?"

"I'll be fine, John. We'll catch up to them."

"I know you will, Harley. But you've got to catch them before the police do."

"Thought you told Nora not to call them. Said so on the phone."

"Now what are the odds of that?"

"I hear you partner. Just leave it to Uncle Buck here."

"Whatever," John said dully. The despair closing his throat. The strangling calamity.

"Things aren't working out?" Harley, both hands on the steering wheel and managing to turn to John between the jolts and bumps. The road ahead all but obliterated by drifting snow.

"No."

"Did you ever think, John, that you might have been a bit optimistic about Luke?"

"Do you think he took Mitch, Harley? Is that what you're trying to tell me?"

"I guess what bothers me, John, is that you set out on this scheme of yours and are prepared to lose your family. It surprises me. And right now all hell could be breaking loose."

"Alright, I fucked up."

"I didn't mean it that way."

"Which way did you mean it then, Harley?" His down-turned mouth.

Harley looked at him hard. Regretful. "Winds picking up," he said. "Damn early for a blizzard. Could use the moisture though."

He leaned forward over the steering-wheel. The landscape all but erased. The ruts he followed were drifting in and seemed shaped from an old and forgotten road. Perhaps a wrong turn.

"Are we on the right road?" John said. Rolled down the window and searched for a landmark. Futile. Scarce on a clear day.

"Hell yeah, the reservoir road is straighter than Albert Triphammer. And I'm going straight."

"Can't see a thing."

"I know where I'm going, John."

"Maybe we should keep on driving, Harley. Just keep on going forever."

"Don't be foolish, John. What we have here is a situation. No time for quitting. You started this. And you're going to have to finish it one way or the other."

"Didn't you try to stop me?"

"Now that's not much use, John. Hell, if Nora couldn't change your mind, I sure wasn't. It was the right thing to do at the time. Doesn't matter if it was right or wrong. To you, it was right. If you want to make another choice, well you can do that too. Every minute a man can make a choice. Does the best he can. Sometimes it doesn't work out the way he figured it would. Other times everything's just fine. This here is full of emotion and personality. Like smoking at a gas pump. If we're smart about it, we can fix this thing."

"Yeah?"

"Sure."

"How?"

"Don't know that yet."

"What kind of talk is that?"

"Faith that some good will come of it."

"Some meaning."

"You could say that."

"You believe that?"

"I do, John. I wouldn't get out of bed if I didn't."

"You seem to like this."

"I don't know if like is the right word. Gets the blood going though, don't it?"

"Watch the road."

chapter
TWENTY SIX

Grandpa Trickett built a hunting shack near the reservoir back in
the days when migrating waterfowl would block the sun in their
numbers. An eclipse of widgeon and teal. He built the shack in an
aspen coulee, the mouth of which emptied into the reservoir. There
where the moisture gathered in the spring and grasses grew rank
and tall and tiger lilies nodded in sunlit glades. A favourite spot for
young John and Luke in the fall when the aspen leaves turned gold
and shimmered and whispered forgotten songs of hunting lore. A
time of prairie nomads. Great rutted paths from the ancient buffalo
herds could still be seen. A marvel to boys who could imagine such
expansive things.

Now the shack was somewhere out in the white swirling world.
The track not so certain and the danger of wind and snow rising as
the temperature dropped. The snow, horizontal fists of it, punching
like an albino pugilist searching out the meek and reckless souls. Up
ahead, John's truck in a snow drift. Evidence to get it out. Footprints
leading away.

A crushing malaise before uncertainty. He felt it before, coming
into Toronto. There he sought some assistance, invoked some plea to
the Great Mystery of the world, a prayer to a God he didn't know but
sensed within him something innate, unerring and real. A prayer to

appease his fear and inspire his courage. Now he prayed for Mitch's safety and Luke's innocence.

"They left the truck," John said. "Should have stuck with it."

"Yeah, they're heading for the shack alright. Damn thing to do, out searching for something they can't see. That's a fact. But I think Mitch knows where he's going, John. He wouldn't have left the truck if he didn't think he could make it. That's the bright side mind you."

"And?"

"This here's one hell of a storm. It's a problem."

"I think we're close to it, Harley."

"Doesn't mean much, John. Men get lost on the way to their barns in such weather."

"And I don't think they're dressed for it."

"That's two strikes against them. We better get after them. Even if Mitch has his directions figured out, a storm like this could get into a man's head, turn him around some. Freeze to death before he could pull his pecker out to piss. And we're not too sure of the situation. What Luke is up to."

Harley grabbed a blanket from behind his seat. Matches and a hatchet. Cut branches from a saskatoon berry bush. John checked his truck and found no clue except an open glove box. It seemed they took the bag of peppermints for food. And the wind made a sound like banshee herdsmen pushing at their backs and stung them with pellets of ice when they turned their cheeks to study the shifting land.

"I'll stay right on your heels, John," Harley said above the screech. "Go ahead slow. If the trail splits up, I'll mark it."

John nodded and lead the way hunched over the dimpled trough of footfall. They both pulled up the collars on their jean jackets. Harley's hat over his ears tighter than stove pipe. Bare weather-beaten hands unaffected. Several times the trails diverged and Harley remained at the fork until John could investigate. Each time one track veered away he soon found that it angled back to join the main trail. It seemed that one doubled back to assist the other. The wind chill was likely having a devastating affect on them. John began to fear that he would come across their drifted bodies prone and dead, their frozen grimaces hating him. Like the death zone on Everest.

And as if such an image could manifest out of the construct of his worried mind, a shape appeared through the white gauze, a prone figure covered in snow, legs splayed behind. He stood before the shape, studied the outline, the clutching of his stomach. Then Harley moved ahead of him and knelt down and brushed away the snow from the legs.

"Pronghorn," he said. Held the cloven hoof for John to see. Gnawed hocks. "Now don't get your mind thinking too much, John. We'll find them. Now let's go. Not far now. Should come to the edge of the coulee any time." Stood up and placed his hand on John's shoulder like a father.

They trudged on following the tracks humped over like gnomes. Then trees appeared as Harley said they would and the trail slipped between the chalky trunks of aspen and down into the coulee away from the slice and howl of weather. In the distance the vague outline of Grandpa Trickett's shack. They stopped on the trail, cautious in the shelter of trees and listened. The snow seemed to have lost its urgency. A gentle falling. Silent against the background of the unfettered prairie rushing over the high crowns.

John turned to Harley, his hat covering his eyes. Frosted nose hairs. "What do you think, Harley?" he whispered.

"Don't see any smoke coming from the shack. Seems odd to me. The first thing I'd do is light a fire in that old stove."

"You alright, Harley?"

"I'm fine. These old frostbitten ears of mine are stinging something fierce. Other than that I'm fine. You?"

"I got a strange feeling that something's not right."

"You think?"

"I don't want to surprise them, Harley."

"Well, we could walk right up to that old shack and knock on the door."

"No, I think we better look through a window first."

"Yeah."

"I just don't know what to expect."

"Just be ready for anything, friend."

"Yeah."

They angled down the slope of the coulee, moving slowly and alert like ambushers. Then a fox cut across in front of them. Stopped in mid-trail and turned and raised a front paw. Smoking breath. Regarded them with circumspect yellow eyes. Then it dropped its paw and padded down the trail a few feet then veered off into a tangle of aspen dead-fall. A glimpse of wild things driven to shelter. They followed the trail of the fox and stood where it disappeared into the thicket. There was no sign of it. John was sure it was watching them from its clever hide. Harley knelt down and touched the spoor like a tracker. No reason for it. Some adventure.

They continued on down the trail. The shack was close now. It seemed to be watching them too. The two windows at the back of it. Big square eyes. John approached the corner of the grey clapboard. Stood breathless. The wind sifting and the sway and knock of trees. Harley inched his way along the side, ducked under a broken window and turned and made eye contact with John. Some kind of signal between men. The time is now.

John removed his hat and crept around the corner and peered into the dark shell with one eye. The slow coming of light and recognition. Mitch on the floor in the corner wrapped in a mattress like a sausage roll. He appeared lifeless. His feet poking out and covered with Luke's jacket. But Luke couldn't be seen. Then John abandoned all caution and rushed passed Harley. "Let's go," he said.

They pushed open the front door and John immediately went to Mitch. He was blue about the lips and his skin marble white and his eyes were closed. A chiseled likeness asleep in a deep-freeze. The thought that Mitch might be dead rushed to every cell of his body, a wave of intense panic, a rippling convulsion that made him queasy and gasp. The collapse of his life. The extinguishing of all meaningless things. He pressed his ear to his lips, desperate to feel a breath.

"No," he said. "No." His thin overwrought voice.

Harley knelt beside him and stuck his hand up inside the mattress like he was birthing a calf. "He's not dead for crying out loud," he said. "I can feel his heart, John."

"God, Harley, be sure."

"No mistake, friend. It's not strong, but he's alive."

"We've got to warm him up, Harley. He's near frozen solid. Get that fire going. Hurry!"

Harley opened the wood-box and it was full of firewood, split and ready for use. The unwritten law of prairie back-country. Soon he had the fire crackling in the stove and heat filled the cold space of the shack. Melted the snow that sifted through the windows. Puddles formed and dripped from the sills. The rank smell of pack-rats rising.

John removed the mattress from around Mitch and let it sprawl on the floor near the stove. He was soaking wet. Jeans stiffened with cold. He peeled off his clothes eased him down on the mattress and covered his milk-white body with Harley' blanket.

"He's hypothermic, John," Harley said. "He's unconscious. One of us needs to get undressed and get under there with him. Use our body heat to bring him around. Saw it on the Discovery Channel."

John glanced around the interior of the dim shack. The wooden bunks and shelves lined with newspaper shredded by mice. A Winchester calender on the wall, a painting of a covey of grouse flushed by a brace of spaniels. John didn't look at the images. Peripheral recognition. They were there as they always had been. What was missing, was Luke.

"Harley, Luke's out there. I have to go after him. And Mitch needs to get warm. I'll never ask you to do another thing. When he's warm enough to travel, we'll get him out of here."

"Don't you worry about Mitch, John. I'll look after him. Just go easy out there. You'll be able to see now. The storm's played out and that cold snap is right behind it. And John, that old .22 of yours is not here. Looks like he has it. It don't mean anything. Just go easy."

From the front door John followed two sets of footprints straight to the reservoir. The trees thinned and the land hollowed and sedges leaned and poked through the snow and all before him was an expanse of ice. No sign of a trail, the grey ice swept of snow, gleamed like polished glass. The prairie returned, appealing and absolute. The beauty of the first snow revealed beneath a blue sky that lifted moods like a drug. But there gashed into the ice, two holes loomed ominous and black several meters apart. As if hit by a meteorite or children lobbing boulders onto a slushy pond. A glazed skin of new ice.

John Trickett moved around the first hole. A long arc creeping. Sliding one foot then the other. Testing. The cracks shooting in all directions. Holding. Then he neared the second hole. The ice sank. Gave under his foot. He couldn't move another inch forward. A hole in the ice and no sign of Luke. He was unwilling to believe that Luke went through. Perhaps a deer. Something else. Or perhaps he managed to crawl back onto the ice. Out there still.

And then something drew his attention beside the hole. A single peppermint. White and perfect. A signature. And the slam of the rifle butt chipped into the ice where Luke must have fallen, where he tried to stop, check himself. The loom of breaking ice. John's knees buckled and the ice yielded to his weight as the image of Luke below him appeared like a nightmare. The drift of him under the ice, frantic to find the hole above him. Hand pressed to the ceiling of ice like a bug in a killing jar. No way out and death approaching cold and swift. The whites of his eyes falling away.

John had to move. There was nothing to do now. He backed away slowly. Tears thickening along his lashes. A salty trickle contained on his cheek. Everything wrong. His will of no use out on the plains

where tragedy was a mere point of view. The unfolding of circumstance. Merle Haggard's, 'rollin' down hill like a snowball headin'
for hell.' For an instant he thought it might be a comfort to break
through the ice and put an end to his ruinous notions for absolution. Just a grievous thought that left him quickly when his attention
returned to Mitch in Grandpa Trickett's shack. And then Steven
Sullivan appeared in his mind. Out of nowhere. Spoke to him.

"Just a dumb fuck, Zeke, to chase the Bug Man out onto the half
frozen ice. No fucking way to make up for abandoning him. Just a
stupid fucking Zeke with Saskatchewan plates. I told you before."

John returned to the shack. It was warm and appealing and he
was relieved to see that Mitch began to move, shiver and tremble
back to life. He opened his eyes.

"Mitch," John said, "can you hear me? It's Dad."

Mitch nodded. Turned his head mechanically to Harley. He
blinked, wondering, then slow-eyed around the shack.

"Gave us quite a scare there, Mitch," Harley said. "Probably
weren't thinking you'd be needing matches." His reassuring smile
glossing over his slight reproach.

"Where's Luke?" Mitch asked sleepily. Jaw and lips like an earth-
quake and turning to Harley beside him. Aghast but tolerant.

The next thought in John Trickett's head. "He's not here, Mitch.
What happened?"

"He went out to the reservoir," Mitch said. "I tried to stop him
but I lost him in the snow. The ice wouldn't hold me and I went
through. I knew I had to get back here. It was so cold. I called out to
him. Then I don't know. I must have managed to crawl out onto solid
ice. Can't remember after that."

He looked down at his son, all of him, seeing him for the first
time in years. Safe and sound and nothing else seemed to matter.
Then a shard of light appeared on the wall like a blessing, expanded,
unveiled the darkness. And out on the reservoir Luke drifted away
from him. Farther still.

chapter
TWENTY SEVEN

The RCMP arrived as John knew they would. A dive team was brought in from Regina and found the .22 in 20 feet of water. It was buried in the soft mud of the reservoir. They couldn't find Luke. Visibility was poor under the ice and the weather turned colder and John was told that they would find Luke in the spring when the ice came off and his body popped to the surface. A dreadful thought that would delay closure on Luke's sad life.

Del and Mitch returned to university. Mitch fully recovered. But before he left Windrush, he said he owed his life to his Uncle Luke. Helped him out there in the blizzard and pulled him out of the frigid hole. "He must have got me out of there," he said. "Thinking about it now, I know I couldn't have done it myself. Carried me back to Grandpa Trickett's shack. He rambled on a bit about things. Seemed muddled. But he wasn't afraid. No, I was in no danger with Uncle Luke. That's the truth."

"What about the rifle, Mitch?" John had asked.

"I took out the old cooey. I wanted to target shoot like I used to. And on the way, I came upon Uncle Luke walking along the Reservoir Road. He didn't say where he was going. And he didn't want to get into the truck at first. But it was blowing pretty bad and finally he got in. Then the weather just got worse."

And through the long winter John Trickett awoke every morning to his chores. Feeding and watering his cattle. Thermos coffee and pissing in the snow. He managed to push his truck on through the drifts to the open side-hill above the reservoir. And at the end of each day he would park there and look out over the frozen water. Stare mostly. Nothing to contemplate save for his foolhardy idea. There was nothing to process in his head with Luke still entombed below him. A sad affair that had to wait the coming spring. Nora was no help with his grieving. She could scarcely speak of the matter herself lest she burst into tears for her harsh views. John Trickett held no grudges, but still all was cheerless about Windrush those months.

Christmas came and went and a fine visit with the boys. Gratitude was palpable around the Trickett table that day and grace was understood to be more than a short prayer before the meal. But that lingering knowing that Luke rest dead and gone below the ice just a few miles from their comforts was a painful distraction. The backdrop to every word and pause. Like the throbbing persistence of a headache aggravated by sudden movement. A laugh would end, trail away and allow the space to be filled with painful gloom. So the chatter rolled on, uninterrupted. Punctuated with glasses of wine. Bottles drained. Corks pried loose from the long necks. But it had to end. Life compelled the rise and set of the sun. Day after day.

And when the call did finally come in early April to tell John that it was time, Nora packed the truck with a blanket, sandwiches, coffee and a saskatoon berry pie. It would be no picnic, but there was no telling how long it would be. She wanted to go along. To be there for John. The RCMP Recovery Team was already on the water. An aluminum boat with dragging hooks. It seemed that Luke's body had not surfaced. There was a chance that it might be snagged on something. Perhaps on an irrigation intake pipe.

John parked his truck where he did all winter. New grass covered the sloping landscape around the reservoir like velvet. A kildeer left its nest, a gravel scrape in the middle of the road in front of the truck. Yellow headed blackbirds in the bullrush. Bird song and fat drifting clouds like wooly sheep passing by. Diamonds on the small lake. The idling chug of an outboard motor. Nora laid the blanket down for them to sit and wait. An outdoor theater. A Canadian Tragedy. A good time for a Gordon Lightfoot song.

John was sick. Lightheaded. The thought of identifying Luke. Six months at the bottom of the reservoir. He had no appetite and wasn't in the mood for talking. He could scarcely bear the tension, the abject horror of the gruesome outcome that would end when the RCMP would signal to him. An arm raised. Come down from the hill to visit upon his brother's demise. A hellish bloated corpse.

"Here, Tim Horton's coffee," Nora said pouring coffee into a cup from the thermos. Looked him over. Worried, but understood his struggle.

"Where did you get that?"

"Harley bought it in Swift Current when he was there on business. He wanted to cheer you up."

"Business?"

"Alright. He made a special trip."

"That old hand. He's one to know the pleasures of a simple man."

"He continues to surprise me."

"Don't know why. He's always been like that." John noticed that the conversation took his mind off of Luke. Momentarily. He felt a measure of relief.

"Just me, then."

John turned to her. Something there. "What is it?"

"See that?" She pointed to the kildeer. "See how she protects her young. Fluttering and flopping as if she had a broken wing. Anything to lure danger away from her nest." She was helping him, gently leading him away from the morose scene of the reservoir.

"Yeah. It's something."

"Do you understand?"

"Yeah, I get it, Nora. You've been reading my book."

"Woman's Search for Meaning."

"That's the one."

Just then a hawk swept low over the slope, wings folded for speed. A shadow racing ahead of it. Suddenly it veered towards the kildeer, but it seemed tentative, uninterested, and sailed on past it and dropped down into the bowl of the reservoir increasing its speed and chances of a kill.

"Did you see that, John?"

"I saw it," he said. "I'm sitting right beside you." Irritated by her obvious attempts to make things right. A correction in the unfolding universe.

"Well, whatever drives that hawk, is in us too. It can't help it. Not a thing it can do about it."

"I know what you're trying to do. Square this thing. You can't. I fucked up. Pure and simple. Told Harley that very same thing."

"Not like you to swear, John."

"Well, it's a good word sometimes. Just seems to fit."

"It doesn't suit you."

"I think the need to swear is a human condition. I'm just trying it out."

"I see."

"All our frustrations. Everyone's got them. That's one thing I learned."

"Do you think we're getting somewhere?"

"Us?"

"Yeah, in all this craziness."

"Maybe. I don't know. I just don't know. What if he committed suicide, Nora, killed himself? Luke knew ice. He just wouldn't walk out onto that lake like that. And if it's true, then I'm responsible. For everything."

"We're getting into some pretty heavy shit, John."

"Sounds like we should consult with Dr. Buck?" A sardonic chuckle.

"Speak of the devil."

Harley's truck came banging up the dirt road. Bounced over potholes. Swerved. Something on his mind. His truck lurched to a stop. He seemed a little rattled as he walked over to the side-hill. Didn't look towards the recovery operation.

"I know you'd be here," he said standing over John and Nora. Fidgeting with something in his hand. Out of breath. Tipped his hat.

"What's going on, Harley?" John said.

"Well, John, this came in the mail this morning." Raised his hand to show them.

"Harley," Nora said, "before you say another word, spit out that wad of horse shit that's tucked under your lip. I don't want to be sprayed by that vile dribble."

Harley reared back. Shook his head then turned and leaned over and spat out his chaw. Glistening turd on the new grass. The passing of his sleeve.

"Thank you," Nora said.

"It's a post card from Toronto," Harley went on, "from you, John. It's all beat up and the ink is smudged. I figured it must have been lost behind a water cooler or something. I wasn't surprised by that fact. You hear of things like that now and then. But I noticed the post mark. It was mailed a week ago, John. From Toronto. And I know you weren't in Toronto last week because you were helping me put that new clutch in my truck. It's the damnedest thing I've ever seen."

John fell against Nora's shoulder. "I forgot to mail it," he said. "It was in my glove-box. He must have…"

"John, are you alright?" Harley said.

He looked up. The boat back and forth stitching the reservoir. "They're not going to find him, are they, Harley?"

Harley paused. His silent speculation. He looked down at his boots then out to the reservoir. Then he strode down the hill and stopped and turned and strode back up. He stood and shook his head in deliberation. "No, not there, friend. It seems he's gone home."

"He wanted us to think he went through the ice," John said. "To give himself time."

"Damn, John. It's just the damnedest thing."

There on the blanket John drew up his knees and folded his arms and rested his head. He was shaking and Nora consoled him. Rubbed his neck. Harley looked on. He was no crier and thrust out his jaw, but it trembled still. A drip at the end of his nose like a jewel and eyes watered and spilled. A sanctuary for his sensitivities.

And down below them the drag boat quit for the day and was loaded onto a trailer and taken away. Then the world turned over to reveal some other world. A new world, fresh and clean, never to be the same. And terns raced over the rippled waters of the reservoir crying, hurry, hurry and clouds moved across the sun and great shadows crept across the prairie like something ephemeral. Then the sun broke through once again and there was only space and tomorrow cradled in the breathing plains.

9 781412 094979

ISBN 1-4120-9497-6